5:58:16

TO DO:
REPORT TO
WORK

W9-BYC-450

The Familiar

Even the book morphs!
Flip the pages
and check it out!

Look for other **ANIMORPHS** ®
titles by K.A. Applegate:

ANIMORPHS

The Familiar

K.A. Applegate

AN
APPLE
PAPERBACK

SCHOLASTIC INC.
New York Toronto London Auckland Sydney
Mexico City New Delhi Hong Kong

Art Direction/Design by Karen Hudson/Ursula Albano
Cover illustration by David B. Mattingly

ISBN 0-439-11515-9

12 11 10 9 8 7 6 5 4 3 2 1   0 1 2 3 4 5 6/0

Printed in the U.S.A.
First Scholastic printing, May 2000

The author wishes to thank Ellen Geroux for her help in preparing this manuscript.

For Michael and Jake

CHAPTER 1

Whummph!

BAAAM!

I slammed the Hork-Bajir into the concrete. Pinned him against the subbasement wall with two massive tiger paws.

His red eyes burned with hatred. His face was a twisted horror as he pushed back, desperate to free his tail blade from behind his body.

I strained to reach the scarred, saddle-leather flesh of his neck. To rip out the throat.

By the way, I'm Jake.

Can't tell you much more than that. Like my last name or where I live. I can't even tell you where I go to school. Here's what I can tell you: Earth is being invaded by parasitic slugs called

1

Yeerks. Still with me? Pretty hard to believe, huh? See, humans seem to be their latest preference in host bodies. They take thousands a day. Make them into slaves. They just squeeze into your ear canal. Wrap themselves around your brain. Tap into your memories and dreams. And then they take over. You can't even decide when to blink. No control at all. It's like your skull becomes a prison. And you're trapped in your own head. No way out.

My friends Marco, Rachel, Cassie, Tobias, an alien kid we call Ax, and I are the only active resistance. So now you're asking yourself, "How are six kids preventing the total takeover of Earth?" Well, we were given the power to turn into any animal we touch. To actually acquire the animal's DNA. To morph. The Andalite technology was a gift to us from Ax's older brother, Elfangor. After he crash-landed, and before he was murdered.

So anyway, we're the only ones fighting back. We managed to slow the Yeerks down a little. But it was getting harder to keep up the fight. Harder to keep it together.

"Hhhhhrrrooooowwwwwrrrr!" I roared.

He faltered and I lunged forward. Missed! His tail broke free and he slashed!

And carved a hole in my underbelly!

I watched, stunned and helpless. Those were *my* guts, spilling from *my* body! I froze up for one

2

instant too long. He pushed me down onto pipes that . . .

Tsssssssssss!

<AHHHHHH!>

My fur was smoking, my flesh scalded!

Adrenaline cracked through my chest like a whip. I was up again, face-to-face with a Yeerk-infested Hork-Bajir.

I had one more chance with this guy. This was it. And suddenly the vividness of the scene seemed to recede.

Don't get me wrong. My guts were still spilling out of my belly. Exhaustion still pressed on my shoulders like a granite slab. But I was in a new zone. It was him or me.

Claws bared, teeth flashing, I leaped.

WHAM!

Heaved him into the wall.

WHAM!

Plowed him into the concrete. His skull hit hard.

WHAM!

His tail dropped. His eyes went lazy, then rolled up into his head. He groaned weakly and slid down the wall.

We were three floors underground, in the dark, dank subbasement of a downtown high-rise. Pipes and ducts ran close overhead. You could hear cries and growls from floor to ceiling and wall to wall. I wheeled around. And only then did I see how insanely bad things were.

We were completely outnumbered.

Cassie was one against two. Marco one on four.

I had to help them!

But I'd drawn a living barrier. Five battle-hardened Hork-Bajir, holding their blades like cocky gunslingers, were closing in on me like the walls of a collapsing room.

Just beyond the Hork-Bajir was what looked like — what I *hoped* was an exit. A steel accordion door thirty feet away, opposite the stairs.

<Everybody out, now! Get to the door!> I yelled, but the other screams and cries and crashes drowned out my words.

<More on the stairs! And Taxxons. I can smell them!> My best friend, Marco. Every quaking syllable told me he was at the end of his strength.

I caught a glimpse of Rachel, hobbling toward the sound of shock troops pouring down the stairs. <Come on!> Her voice cracked. Blood gushed from gashes around her eyes, blinding her. <Where are they?!> She slashed her grizzly bear paws wildly.

<Rachel, no!>

Three Hork-Bajir struck. Ran her across the room like a football-tackling dummy.

"TSEEER!"

Tobias swooped and plunged, talons first. One Hork-Bajir fell off, clutching his eyes. Cassie clamped on to another's heel and yanked her steel-trap jaws from side to side.

Rachel was still helpless.

I backed up nervously. I was surrounded, closed off from the others by the approaching Hork-Bajir barricade. My butt hit the concrete wall.

I reared up and roared. Seven hundred pounds of ripping claws and slicing teeth. Fluid strength. Mercurial speed. The male Siberian tiger. The biggest cat in the world.

But my roar echoed back unmasked. I heard false confidence. I detected despair.

"Ghafrash nyut!" said a voice like gravel. "Die!"

The nearest Hork-Bajir lunged, blades flashing.

Mouth open, I leaped. My fangs sank in deep, past the armor of skin. Into the meat.

He jerked back and fell under my weight. I rolled off and slammed to the floor. My right ear! Still stuck to his wrist blade! Sliced off!

Two more were on me. I'd forgotten any thought of victory. Now it was simply a mindless struggle. A blade embedded in my left hind leg . . . *Focus, Jake. Survive.*

FWAAP!

5

A tail blade cleaved the air above me. Blue fur.

It was Ax.

Fwaap, fwaap, fwaap!

Two assailants slumped and crumpled to the floor. A third screamed and cradled his knees.

<Prince Jake, if we do not leave now, we never will.>

Movement.

<Ax!> I cried. <Hit the floor!>

Ax ducked. The bladed body of a Hork-Bajir whistled through the air.

Then there was a fierce metallic crash and hiss.

Pssssssssshhhhhttttt!

A cracked steam pipe! An explosion of steam! Pressurized fog billowed across the floor. It enveloped the room, everyone and everything. Confusion took over.

Now or never.

<Now!> I ordered. <Bail!> It was impossible to see more than an inch ahead. The scalding cloud burned my skin and eyes and throat. Choking on steam, bodychecking Hork-Bajir, I ran for the parking garage door and slammed my bloody mass on the weight-sensitive panel. The door began to creak open, inching up at first, then rising rapidly. Six inches, twelve inches, eighteen.

Cassie squeezed out through the opening. Then Ax. Tobias.

<I'll kill them!> It was Rachel's voice. Raving like someone possessed. <Get your hands off me, Marco! I'll kill them! I'll kill them!>

<Shut the door, Jake!> Marco roared. <There are more on the stairs!>

<Marco, Rachel, get out of here now!>

<We can't. Rachel's . . . can't leave her. You cut the Yeerks off or it'll be too late!> He was breathless, but insistent. <We'll find some other way out.>

A Hork-Bajir emerged from the steam cloud, saw me, and broke into a run. Time was definitely not on my side today.

Lose everyone, or lose two?

I dropped and rolled under the door, sprang up and broke the glass box that housed the emergency close switch. Engaged the switch.

What alternative did I have? What choice?

The door ground to a halt, hesitated, then changed directions, descending like a slow but certain guillotine. Cassie's wolf eyes fixed on me.

<What are you doing? You can't trap them in there. You can't leave them!>

CHAPTER 2

The lone Hork-Bajir dove and skidded under the door. I grabbed him, mouth and claws. We tumbled. It was like being stuffed in the clothes dryer with ten razor-sharp kitchen knives.

I used my weight, my fangs, the last of my strength. When his muscles finally slackened, I stumbled away. The accordion door was almost closed.

I looked through the crack and there, like a mirage, was Marco's gorilla form emerging from the steam cloud. He was dragging a roaring, slashing Rachel. And not more than six feet behind them, a dozen Hork-Bajir.

Ax grabbed a length of pipe and wedged it between the floor and door. The gears shrieked to a crawl.

Then the pipe began to bend.

Cassie screamed.

The crunching metal door was just inches from the floor when thick, black fingers wrapped around the bottom. And with inconceivable strength, Marco heaved it up. Forced Rachel through. She was a bloody mess.

Marco stooped, crawled under the door, and released the pipe. Four Hork-Bajir dove for the opening. Slid, clattered, reached the door just as . . .

BOOM!

It crashed shut. No Hork-Bajir made it through. In one piece, anyway.

<Demorph!> I yelled.

We raced up the empty, spiral parking ramp.

I demorphed as I ran. Orange-, white-, black-, and red-striped fur thinned to a fuzz, then disappeared. My tail shrank into my coccyx. The guts that hung from my belly were drawn back in.

Bones shifted, rearranged, and threw me onto my hind legs. I tripped and stumbled against the wall. My front legs were absorbed and then reissued as human arms. Back legs extended, paws minimized, claws grew into toes and fingers.

"Let's get out of here!"

We plateaued onto level pavement, our trans-formations complete. We sprinted, breathless, down a row of parked cars. Shot past a dumb-founded attendant who saw a hawk and five kids in spandex tear into a downtown street.

A busy downtown street.

"Look out!"

Honk! Honk!

Drivers slammed on their horns. Cars screeched to a halt.

I jumped back between parked cars on the side of the street. Rachel and Marco ran for the sidewalk.

"Cassie!"

She was in the middle of the street, frozen.

I ran back into the lanes. A driver opened his car door. "Punks!" He shook his fist. "Bunch of no good . . ."

I grabbed Cassie's arm. Yanked her out of traffic. Dodged into the alley where Marco and Rachel had turned in, following Ax.

"Cassie!" I shook her roughly. She came to.

"Four of them," she said anxiously. "I may have killed four back there, maybe five." She searched my eyes, her usual calm shattered. "Jake!" she whispered. "How do I deal with this?"

I gently pushed her down along the alley,

shushing her, and looking back over my shoulder. The Yeerks could still be on the trail.

"Every day we're more like them," she persisted. "Aren't we?" Tears welled over her lower lids. "Jake?"

I didn't have the energy for this. The doubt, the introspection, the analysis. I just didn't have the energy.

"No," I said flatly.

Why was she doing this? Why now? Yeah, we'd just had one of the closest calls I could remember. We'd had to scrap the mission and now the new Yeerk-pool entrance would open on schedule. But the brutality was nothing we hadn't done a hundred times before.

She began to cry almost noiselessly. I knew she needed to talk things over. She needed to work through the confusion we all feel after a battle and she wanted me to help.

But I walked away.

Marco and Rachel were up ahead, farther down the alley.

"You're wrong!" Rachel cried, still pumped. "I could have brought them all down." Her fist slammed the Dumpster. Marco kicked it even more violently.

"You had blood in your eyes! You couldn't even see the reinforcements swarming down the

11

stairs. You acted like an idiot. A selfish, crazy, whacked-out . . ."

"Relax," I said, stepping between them like the leader I was supposed to be. Marco didn't listen.

"You're about to blow, Rachel." His face was bright red, hot from exertion and frustration. "Haven't you learned *anything*? You put everyone at risk by hanging back when Jake said to bail. We can't always cater to your personal need to bash heads."

"But as long as we follow Marco's righteous program, everything's fine?" She picked up an empty can and heaved it across the alley. "Mighty Marco can just . . ."

"Forget about saving your life next time?"

"I said *relax*!" I shouted.

There was a sudden rustling on the far side of the Dumpster. We tensed instantly.

Around the corner peeked a boy, an oddly good-looking kid.

Rachel gave a snort.

It was Ax, in human morph.

"I have not heard from Tobias," Ax said to me.

"Try again. Ask him if we're clear."

I looked up at the strip of late-evening sky visible from the alley. A raptor's form floated over then disappeared behind a glassy high-rise.

"Oh, that's really great! What a guy. So he's off the clock now?" Marco walked around behind the Dumpster and began to morph. "I'm going home."

I kept watching the sky. Rachel, already morphed to bald eagle, powered her body up past the bricks. I knew she was going after Tobias. Ever since a Yeerk sub-visser held and tortured him, Tobias hadn't been the same. Even more time spent alone now than before. Withdrawn, despondent.

Not good.

"Prince Jake," Ax said. "Should we meet in the barn tonight and attempt the mission again tomorrow?"

I sighed. Cassie's sobs were intermittent now. She rose from the pavement, from the shadow of a pile of cardboard boxes, and walked slowly toward the street.

"I don't know, Ax," I said, watching Cassie. "Will you do me a favor, though? Will you make sure she gets home okay?"

CHAPTER 3

I headed home alone.

I demorphed in a tree in my front yard. I knew it was risky, being so close to the house and all, but I was drunk with exhaustion. When I dropped to the grass, my legs went limp under me.

The gravel stabbed my bare feet as I staggered up the path. The porch light was on. The other lights out.

I paused with my hand on the doorknob and glanced down at my body. Spandex bike shorts and tight T-shirt. I looked like I should be giving a testimonial on a Tae Bo infomercial. I had regular clothes stashed in the garage. I needed to put them on.

The garage. It seemed so far away. I was so tired, my muscles ached . . .

I pushed open the door. Forget about my normal clothes. My parents, if they were home, would probably just think this morphing outfit was some new fashion. You know — something Rachel thought up. Well, she says this is cutting edge or something.

My brother Tom, my brother with a Yeerk in his head, would never buy that one.

But Tom wasn't home. Friday night meant he was at The Sharing. The front organization for Controllers.

I opened the fridge, grabbed a leftover slice of pizza, and started to stuff my face. I left the kitchen to climb the stairs to bed. One, two, three . . . I could feel it already, my head hitting the pillow, sleep descending. Dreams would come. No nightmares. Just dreams of . . .

"Jake?"

My head snapped up. A piece of pizza crust lodged in my throat.

The voice was loud and mocking. "Bare feet? You been riding your bike barefoot? At night?"

It was Tom. He stood at the top of the stairs. Tall and confident. Blocking my path. Guess it was a quick night at The Sharing.

I coughed, hacking up the pizza crust.

"Hey," I said, forcing a half-smile. "I, uh . . . I was over at Marco's. Watching the game. It went into overtime and, well, Detroit scored and Marco jumped up and smacked a Pepsi all over my jeans and sneakers. I left them there to get washed."

"Yeah?" Tom said, frown fading. "Well, you look pretty stupid. But that's really not unusual, is it?" He was smirking now.

"Whatever," I ran up the rest of the stairs and jabbed him in the stomach, the way a little brother would.

He fell to the floor, feigning injury, but hooked my foot and tripped me as I walked into my room.

We laughed.

"I'm gonna crash," I said, recovering my balance. "I'm beat."

"Yeah. Fine." He headed for his room. Did he buy it? Did he believe the lies I'd grown so used to telling? The fake-nice routine I put on for a brother who's not a brother at all anymore, but the enemy?

I dropped into bed. Pulled the blanket up to my neck. Began to shut my . . .

A noise in the doorway.

I shot up. Flicked on the lamp.

"Hey, Midget?" Tom poked his head around my door frame. "Was that blood on your leg?"

My breathing stopped.

Sometimes, when you demorph, the blood of battle stays behind.

"Uh." My voice faltered. My brain slowed. "You know about my bike. It stinks. The stupid chain catches my skin. I should get Dad to buy me a new one." I dropped back onto my pillow. Switched off the light.

Waited.

Tom let it go.

But when I glanced once more at my bedroom doorway, Tom's shadow was still there. Did he have something more to say?

I was too tired to ask. Sleep was dragging down my eyelids.

Whatever it was could wait till morning.

Eyes closed, I saw Cassie. Watched her solitary figure walking down the alley. Away from me. Toward a busy street where cars flashed past.

I saw Tom's leery eyes. Always watching. Policing. Scheming. Eyes controlled by the very small, but very real parasitic slug in his brain. The Yeerk. The race of alien invaders, pressing ever forward in stealthy conquest of humanity.

And suddenly, I stood before a giant wall, rising leagues above my head and running for miles in both directions. I had my hand crammed

17

against a small hole, from which water slowly seeped and bubbled. On the other side I heard the raging sea. Pummeling. Pounding. Weakening, with each lashing, every fiber of the wall.

And I wondered: Just how long would it hold?

CHAPTER 4

$\square$E-DEET! DE-DEET!

The alarm was like a jackhammer to the head. I groaned.

DE-DEET!

Enough, already! I felt for the clock radio. The snooze button. Just five more minutes.

My hand patted the air. No bedside table? I lifted my lids. Where was my . . .

My heart stopped.

I was staring into a triangular screen. A flat computer panel mounted flush in a peeling, white plaster wall across from the bed. Eerie copper letters pulsed at the top of the glowing gray screen. 5:58:16 A.M. Below the time flashed the

19

words "TO DO" and a single entry: "Report to work."

This was not my bedroom. Not even close.

DE-DEET! DE-DEET!

My body stiffened to defense mode and I bolted out of bed.

The alarm stopped.

My mind, forced into consciousness by the shock, hurled me orders. *Get out!* it warned. *Get out, get out, get out!*

I raced to a tall black panel in the wall. A door. Had to be.

Get out!

I tried, but there was no handle. No release lever. Nothing.

I struck it.

"You are not prepared to leave for work!" said a shrill computer voice.

I pounded even harder. Hammered the panel with a clenched fist. A fist that . . .

I stopped suddenly as I studied my fist. It was big.

I mean it was rough and callused and had veins that pumped across the hairy, muscular forearm like I belonged to Gold's Gym and actually used my membership.

It was the hand and arm of a grown man.

My heart started up again, pumping now at record speed.

I probed the polished steel door frame for my reflection, for the face I knew.

And yes, there! I saw my eyes, dark as midnight. My strong, broad face. My . . .

I swallowed hard.

My short-cropped hair? My six-foot frame?

My day-old beard?!

I brought a hand to my face. My fingers scraped across my chin. Stubble like sixty-grit sandpaper. I needed a shave.

My breath got choppy. My head felt about ready to explode.

The Jake staring back at me was an adult! Not crazy old. But out of college a few years. At least ten years older than the kid I'd been the night before.

What was going on? Where were the others? How did I get to this place?

My heart was beating entirely too hard.

I was gonna have a heart attack if I didn't calm down. I stumbled back to bed and sat down on the narrow strip no wider than a torso. A pad on a metal plate.

"Okay," I said out loud. "Okay." Use your brain. Cover the possible explanations.

An Ellimist trick? Yeah, it had to be. But why hadn't he spoken?

A Yeerk experiment, maybe? Could I have been captured?

It's hard to think straight when you wake up like Tom Hanks in that movie *Big.* At least he woke up in his own room, in his own clothes. Sort of. I was wearing this weird, faded orange jumpsuit, the color of a sun-bleached Orioles cap.

I fingered the suit, and then it hit me.

Of course!

I knew what was going on here. It had finally happened.

I knew it was only a matter of time, what with the pressures of leadership, the violent battle, the endless fights against a strengthening enemy.

I'd finally been driven to a complete psychotic breakdown.

I'd gone crazy.

And this was my padded cell.

CHAPTER 5

It really was a cell. Maybe twelve by twelve. But it didn't look very institutional. What it looked like was the remodeling job from hell. A bizarre fusion of decaying early-century architecture and modern metallic installations.

Two walls of bubbling plaster rose twelve feet to a carved crown molding. An old porcelain sink basin stuck out in one corner. Hardwood flooring ran underfoot and spilled over into filthy yellow linoleum about halfway across.

Applied over all this old stuff was a second phase of construction. Brightly colored metallic retrofits sprouted from two gray, synthetic walls. I stood up and walked toward a purple, kidney-shaped pedestal. The top slid off to reveal a golden cone. It was decorated — I guess — with a border of luminescent tubing.

Flit, flit, flit. Sheets of soft paper shot at me from a slit in the wall and floated to the floor.

Flit, flit, flit. More paper.

Whoooosh!

A violent suction nearly pulled my pant leg down the cone. The luminous tubing dimmed. The kidney lid slid shut.

"Evacuation complete!" said the jarring computer voice. I almost smiled. Whoever or whatever held me prisoner here was powerful, but they had a toilet that was out of order.

I moved to a tray colored brilliant fuchsia. It sat beside an electric blue cylinder. Ghastly stalks retracted the tubes into the wall as I walked closer.

Whoop. Bam.

I stared.

Whoop. Bam.

They reappeared, steaming with crisp bacon and scrambled eggs. Orange juice swirled in a blue beaker.

I certainly wasn't hungry.

I moved on to a long, narrow panel, solid but translucent. Faint natural light shone through it. My pulse quickened. A window? Maybe I could escape that way.

Shleep!

The wall absorbed the panel and revealed an

opening three inches wide. A sliver of window. Heavy, cool air tunneled in and caressed my face. I pressed my eyes closed, then opened them, and there . . .

Structures, hundreds of them, rose beneath me, soared above me. Glass, steel, concrete, masonry. All jutting toward a simmering, red-cast sky.

An urban jungle.

But just like my cell, the city looked as though it had suffered modifications at the hands of a deranged contractor. Chaotic clumps of black machinery clung, like unwelcome growths, to the skyscrapers' sides. Sickly deformations of a century's architectural monuments.

A few buildings were completely covered over by this industrial appliqué, like a ship's hull overrun with barnacles. A tree trunk strung with parasitic . . .

The word left me with a very uneasy feeling.

Parasitic . . .

Two fighters zoomed into my narrow field of vision. Their red lights blazed a streak across the cityscape.

Oh. Crap.

Yeerk fighters.

They headed for a distant pack of skyscrapers, an ominous elevation that studded the horizon like giant chipped and broken teeth in the

25

mouth of some mythical hockey goalie. Two of the buildings looked familiar. Shimmering rectangles. Twin towers.

The World Trade Center!

New York. This must be . . . except for . . .

Yeerk fighters out in the open? That meant . . . that meant they'd launched an open attack. Visser Three. They'd gained enough forces to forget stealth and secrets, and wage a totally in-your-face war!

DE-DEET! DE-DEET!

The alarm sounded again.

"Facility air quality jeopardized!" The computer voice was more authoritative now. The window cover began to shut, closing off my sliver of city.

Oh, no you don't! I reached up and grabbed the panel. Forced it back.

One of those fighters wasn't Yeerk.

Only one was a Bug fighter. Only one was a legless cockroach with two serrated spears.

The other held its shredder raked high over the fuselage, pointing forward. Like an Andalite tail poised for combat.

It was an Andalite craft. But grossly modified. Engines that should have glowed a cool blue instead burned a fiery red.

I fought the window cover. I had to see!

The two fighters rocketed through the sky.

They buzzed through the sticky, filmy cloud that swelled above the city like fallout from a colossal explosion.

"Continued idleness prohibited!" The sharp computer voice broke through the monotonous, mind-filling hum from outside.

The fighters banked in tandem, slowed and hovered. Touched down on a platform connecting the World Trade towers.

I let the window cover slam shut.

There was no war being waged after all.

The war, it seemed, was over.

CHAPTER 6

Tssssst.

The cell door opened and ejected me with a burst of air into the dim hallway of an old apartment house. I heard the hiss of other panel doors opening and closing at the same time. Tall, fit humans dressed in brightly colored jumpsuits swarmed into the corridor.

I wanted to yell. I wanted to grab the nearest person and shake him and scream, "What is this crazy place?"

But instinct told me to keep my mouth shut. *Find the answers yourself,* it said. *Observe. Don't trust these strangers. Use them.*

I let the orange and green and yellow suits sweep me up in their mass exodus down the hall.

The wind grew stronger. The ghostly whir and hum I'd heard through the cell window churned louder and louder, until at last it vibrated every particle of air like a thousand-piece orchestra of different-sized fans.

The building wall at the end of the hall had been knocked out. Everyone was stepping through the rough opening. And I followed — curious and terrified — out onto the crowded, open-air docking bay.

"Step up!" An impersonal computer voice cut through the whoosh of engines and flooded my ears. I realized I was blocking traffic.

I tripped forward toward a line of SUV-sized craft that hovered in the air at floor level, doors open, inhaling small groups of colored jumpsuits. And every few seconds . . .

Woooooosh!

One took off from the apartment building and fell away in a controlled tumble, careening toward the streets three hundred feet below.

I stumbled past the blinking red lights that ran from nose to tail on every craft and bathed the docking bay and passengers in a sinister, pulsing glow. Stepped into what looked like a stripped-down Bug fighter. No weaponry or combat stations. Just a pod with seats and windows. A floating, high-tech subway car.

The instant I fell onto a seat, a belt shot

across my chest. Another drew tight over my legs. Before I could panic . . .

Shoo-shoo-shoo.

The unmanned hovercraft drew power. A deep computer voice boomed, "Midtown express." Doors clicked shut and . . .

Sheeeeeeooo!

Into an aerial roll! Hanging upside down! My stomach went goofy. Gray high-rises shot past. Other hovercraft streaked past the windows.

"Hey." A human voice cut through the hum.

We banked right. Flipped a sudden 180 degrees. And leveled off, upright, soaring parallel to the street grid below.

"Hey, Essak-Twenty-Four-Twelve-Seven-Five!" The male voice was friendly. I felt a hand on my shoulder. I flinched, but turned.

A guy in a green suit, strapped to the seat to my left, stared at me with icy blue eyes. Green Suit was talking to me!

My heart hammered. My head began to pound.

"When's the launch?" he said.

I stared blankly back at him, unable to speak as we traced a slalom course between buildings.

The launch? What launch?

Air brakes rose to a frenzied roar. The hovercraft grazed a landing dock. The computer voice boomed, "Middle management!" Everyone suited in green rose and filed out.

Green Suit flashed a mischievous smile. "Mr. Hotshot Scientist forget to have his coffee?"

He disappeared into the crowd. The doors clicked closed.

That green suit . . . that green suit had called me by what I knew had to be a Yeerk name.

CHAPTER 7

We shot high. Skimmed the tops of tall towers. The Chrysler Building filled the windows. Streamlined and whimsical, just like in the photo my mom had in her office. All rounded edges and gleaming stainless steel and . . .

Wait a minute. I looked closer and saw it was covered in some kind of sack. A silver sheath, draped like a giant deflated gift balloon. Busy workers moved about on platforms jutting from the skin at all levels.

My mind was swimming . . .

Even the Chrysler Building. Transformed.

Swimming . . .

That green suit had called me by a Yeerk name . . .

I wasn't Yeerk. How could I be? What was going on?

When a Yeerk slug slithers through your ear canal, when it melds and flattens into every crevice of your brain, you know it's happening. Trust me, you know. Because you can't eat or talk or call up memories unless the Yeerk lets you. You're a helpless observer of an endless nightmare. A prisoner in your own head.

I was no prisoner. My eyes moved freely. My legs, when they weren't strapped to a hovercraft seat, walked where I told them to walk. Why wouldn't whoever was responsible for this just talk to me?

Until today, I'd been the leader . . .

No! I still was the leader of a small but powerful resistance to the Yeerk invasion. A group of six kids, five humans and an Andalite. We call ourselves Animorphs because of our secret weapon, the power to morph into any animal we touch. We fight the Yeerk invaders, led by Visser Three. Those slimy parasitic aliens who've come to Earth to enslave our bodies because without host bodies, Yeerks aren't much more than the wriggling, helpless worms you avoid on the sidewalk after it rains.

There was no Yeerk in my brain. I was no human-Controller.

Not Essak-Twenty-Four-whatever.

No! It's . . .

33

"Jake! My name is Jake!"

The words slipped out before I could stop them. Pierced the relative silence of the cabin.

"What's the matter with you?" said a yellow-suit with an accent. Eight pairs of eyes fixed on me. Eight faces I might have taken to be your average, ethnically diverse, cross section of New York commuters.

Emphasis on "might have."

Because there was one crucial giveaway.

They'd reacted to me.

See, I'd been to New York before. A class trip. I may not have noticed much of the cultural stuff I was supposed to have noticed, but I noticed one thing. You can shout Hamlet's soliloquy or scream Limp Bizkit lyrics, you can blare "The Star-Spangled Banner" or stomp an American flag, and no one — I mean no one — will give you the time of day. They'll look you over, but then they'll walk right on.

All I'd said was, "My name is Jake." And these guys were on me like I'd driven a Kawasaki into their living rooms.

I forced a smile. These weren't New Yorkers. These were human-Controllers. These were Yeerks.

Watch your step, Jake.

I cleared my throat. "My host," I said. "Sometimes I still . . . have trouble. You know, controlling him."

The craft stopped again. "Medicine," the computer voice declared.

"They have pills for that now," Yellow Suit answered. "You should visit the clinic."

He rose and shuffled out. Seven other yellow suits filed out after him. The doors closed. We twisted away from the landing dock. Just me and one other orange suit.

A short ride.

"Research and development. End of the line." The orange suit questioned me when I didn't rise.

"Going to the clinic," I said smoothly. "Not well." I pointed at my head. She gave me a look of understanding. The doors closed behind her.

I was alone.

"My name is JAKE!" I yelled. And then I yelled it again.

And for a second, I thought I would lose it. Really lose it. Start screaming stuff like, "I don't wear jumpsuits, I wear jeans! I'm not twenty-five, I'm a kid! I'm not a Controller, I'm free."

But I didn't. Chances were that someone, somewhere, was watching. At least that's what my gut told me. I've learned to trust my gut.

Down, down, down. The craft fell like a parachute, bobbing slightly with the buffets of wind, descending slowly toward street level.

I looked out over a small park. A fraction the size of Central Park. Trampling the crusty, late-winter grass was a mass of bodies. Blue and tan fur. Hooves. Stalk eyes. The bodies were assembled in orderly, disciplined rows. Maybe fifty across and a hundred lengthwise.

A fog horn blared and they stopped and turned, changing directions.

Captive Andalites. And they were feeding.

My spine felt like a live lightning rod. A world with Andalite-Controllers is no world at all.

In the world I know there is only one Andalite-Controller. And he's a sad mistake. Any conscious Andalite warrior would use his tail blade on himself before he'd let himself be captured.

The craft buzzed just feet above the street, passing rows of blacked-out windows on run-down facades. The ship entered a large, open space. A sort of parking lot. A paved triangle filled with other hovercraft. The engines were cut. The craft docked.

I didn't know what world this was. I didn't know what time this was. A world before or after or parallel to mine? A bizarre reality that had somehow imposed itself on the one I was used to accepting?

My own personal nightmare?

I didn't know. But I knew the Yeerks were strong in this place. They owned this city. They owned the people in it.

But they didn't own me.

36

As long as I was free and in control of my mind, there was a chance — no — the certainty that I could find out what was going on.

And then maybe, just maybe, somehow — even in this strange place — I could find the others and together we could . . .

The doors opened and I dropped to the concrete. My heart was back to its regular rhythm. My mind calmed and focused on a single thought.

"Jake," I breathed quietly, "you didn't plan this one, but now it's time to deal."

CHAPTER 8

Ever imagine a scenario where world leaders lose their minds, fire up those intercontinental ballistic missiles and nuke the whole planet? Ever think what it would be like to step out of the shelter, after the worst of the residue cleared, into some kind of postapocalyptic wasteland?

Well, there I was, stepping out into the wasteland of Times Square. The desolate ground zero of some neutron bomb. A stage set, minus the cast of characters. The whole place coated in menacing silence.

Sure, five hundred feet overhead roared a Yeerk metropolis. But down here, down at street level . . . no taxis clanking over manhole covers. No kamikaze bike messengers daring traffic. No giddy groups of camera-toting tourists. No sharply dressed natives surging like lemmings in and out of high-rises.

The only life was the buzz of giant, electrified billboards a hundred feet overhead. You know, those big, bold ads that make Times Square famous? I scanned. Not even close to the endorsements for Coca-Cola or JVC or Calvin Klein I remembered.

"You can go home again." The words flickered like an electrical storm above the image of a darkened planet. What looked like thick, headless cattle roamed beneath the words against a puke-green sky. Sickly, low-lying trees grew horizontally, like lengthy fingers of barbed wire. "Tired of the city?" another billboard read. "Make the Yeerk home world your home, too. Transports leaving noon and midnight, first of each cycle, Yeerk Empire State Building."

And at the bottom, in smaller print, were the words "High Council Division for the Relocation of Unfit and Insurrectionist Hosts." These words were sprayed over by the graffiti tag "EF."

I stopped in my tracks. The tagger's letters weren't some preconquest relic. They were new. They were fresh. They were angry.

Unfit and Insurrectionist Hosts?

A tinge of hope swelled against the well-anchored caution and fear in my mind. Was there

39

a rebellion going on here? A resistance group somewhere? If I had allies in this town, I had to find them.

But I needed to find the others first. They had to be here, too, right? Only where? In normal NYC, Marco could be in any video arcade in Manhattan, Rachel in any Express from Midtown to SoHo. I looked at the busted-up storefronts and littered streets. Were there parts of the ground-city that still functioned normally? I wasn't ready to bet on it.

All at once I realized Cassie would be easiest to find. A park. She'd be in a park and I'd seen one of those. She'd be feeding the pigeons and . . .

BAMBAMBAMBAMBAMBAMBAMBAM!

I hit the ground.

BAMBAMBAMBAMBAMBAMBAMBAM!

Machine-gun fire. I rolled behind a kiosk and searched for the source.

TSEEEW! TSEEEW!

Dracon fire return, followed by a piercing human cry. A shoot-out at the other end of Times Square? The echo of weapon fire died away and was replaced by a clacking. A clicking. Clawed feet scratching over concrete. Weird, half-whistled words . . .

"Sssssssnit waaanaaa!" The loud, arrogant rasping drew snickering agreement from slobbering mouths.

I edged around the kiosk, and sure enough . . .
Taxxons.

A gang of them. Six or eight. Swaggering up
from Forty-Second Street, straight toward me. Ban-
doliers of energy ammo and handheld Dracon-
beams crisscrossed their massive centipede bodies.
Horrific scars striped their bloated chests.

I fought the urge to sprint. I needed to play
the part of a Controller, and a Controller wouldn't
run. But I had to get away! I was out of place at
ground level. As far as I could see, I was the only
human on the street and it didn't take long to
guess why that might be. No Taxxon encounter
had ever ended well. Why expect something
new?

Where to go?

The McDonald's on the corner was a burned-
out shell. The golden arches lay crushed and dim
on the sidewalk. I'd be a sitting duck.

The high-rise lobby was all glass. No cover.

Suddenly.

"TSSEEERRR!"

A raptor's cry. A swishing of wings. Out of
nowhere! A red-tailed hawk buzzed my head. He
looked ancient. Thin, with feathers missing and
skin taut around the eyes. He sailed into the
steam cloud over a subway grate.

I blinked . . .

Gone. He was gone!

"Tobias?"

No answer. A mirage?

"Ssssreee sreeenaaaa!"

I jerked back. I'd stepped out from behind the kiosk. The Taxxon gang leader had spotted me. Claw arms skittered. His speed increased to an all-out lumber.

CHAPTER 9

Steam. The subway. Go!

I ran for the subway entrance and took the steps three at a time. Wham! I burst through the rusted-out gate.

"Ugh!" A horrible stench. A humid rot. The foul scent of . . . Taxxons.

I gasped for breath in the hot stink of the cavern.

"Who are you?"

"Yahh!" I almost had another heart attack. My head slammed the scissored turnstile in surprise.

A guy, a human, only three feet tall but an adult, looked up at me quizzically. He whipped the

43

stack of flyers he was carrying behind his back. I thought I saw the letters "EF," but I wasn't sure.

"What'd you do to get sent down here?" The way he said it freaked me out. Like some jury had sentenced me to a horrible fate.

I was still struggling for breath.

The guy shrugged and continued. "You won't last long down here. No one does."

I heard the gate bang open one flight up. The sound of skittering Taxxon feet. The little guy's eyes widened. He turned and ran.

I followed.

Down a white-tiled tunnel that narrowed and narrowed until my shoulders scraped the sides. Then into a still smaller channel that brought me to my knees. I crawled wildly through dampness. The Taxxon war cries grew fainter. Then, a new sound. Weak moans and muffled cries that filled the almost total darkness.

We emerged into a wide, domed hall with a stagnant, toxic puddle at its center. Clustered around this shallow, filthy water — cramped and miserable — was a sampling of human and alien life.

A horrific sampling.

Clumsy Gedds loped along at a snail's pace. Battered Hork-Bajir, missing arms or legs or both, huddled around a glowing pit. Human children, and maimed or disabled adults, lay on thin, soiled mats. Battle-scarred Andalites, some minus tail blades and others without stalk eyes, milled restlessly. The stench was profound. The moans were heartrending.

It was the eyes that told the story, though. Defeated, dejected. Living death.

At the sound of our abrupt entrance, most turned and tensed. Weak as they were, they were ready to run. Not fight. That was clear.

"What is this?" I gasped. "Who are you?" The fumes made me light-headed.

The little guy interrupted his whispers of reassurance to a group of human kids. "Depends who you ask," he said. "The Emperor calls us fugitives. The EF calls us refugees. I call us casualties. Casualties of the Fitness Policy. But it doesn't really matter, does it? We're all prey." He smiled. "Your body is strong. You must suffer mental illness?"

I could hardly argue. "I must."

"Ah." His tone turned gentler, more condescending. "Take heart, friend. At least with your strong body you stand a chance against the Taxxon Special Force. With our help, you may last a month. Perhaps even two."

My vision was wigging out. The little guy's face seemed to approach and recede. The stench was eating away my brain. I moved back toward the tunnel and began to scrabble through.

"No," he cried, alarmed. "You must stay with us. Alone you won't last two hours!"

I had to get above ground. I was desperate for air. I was going to pass out.

Back down the tunnel. Left turn, left again. Onto the platform of a subway station. The light was dim and reddish.

Suddenly . . .

Massive suction!

I was being pulled toward the rails by an intense, all-consuming suction! I had to fight against it!

I ran for the exit, but I was barely moving forward. Like that horrible nightmare where your legs feel like fifty-pound weights. Or you're running through water.

I looked down at the rails ten feet below. They were covered in a dirt-packed ooze, seething and twisting with Taxxons!

It was a living stream of Taxxons. Traveling, legs pulled in. Being sucked like lugers along an underground highway, red eyes jiggling as they flew past.

This was Taxxon Mass Transit.

And I was six feet from being sucked in with them!

"Ahh!"

THWAP! thaap!

THWAP!

Two Taxxons rolled out of the suction stream. Lumbered onto the platform! Mouths full of razor-sharp teeth snapped for me. Hundreds of clawed feet powered toward me.

Noooo!

I grabbed for a bench and pulled myself closer to it, fighting the intense suction. Then past it. I grabbed for the trash can bolted to the floor, pulled myself past. Column! Bench! Sign! Trash can!

I looked over my shoulder. The Taxxons were struggling against the suction, too, but they were bigger and they knew something I didn't. They had dropped to the floor and were slinking along. Racing like salamanders.

Bench! Column! Column! Pull!

They would overtake me.

Gate!

I flung it open. The exit stairs! I strained. I reached.

"Ahhhhhhhhhh!"

Something cut into my leg. I twisted. Jammed a fist into an airbag chest. Slammed the gate on gaping jaws and a probing tongue.

Then I clambered toward daylight. Up, up,

up. Sweating. Gasping. Leg nearly crippled with pain. Head throbbing from running into the turn-stile.

The street! The pavement!

Gasping breath after breath of fresh air, I col-lapsed.

Rolled onto my back. And froze.

I wasn't alone.

CHAPTER 10

"Gehhhtuupoorraanjjsoooot!"

Words like a waterfall of syllables, strung tightly together.

Totally incomprehensible.

"Wutryoodooingindtheaghetoo?"

Okay. This was a dream. That was the only possible explanation. But what felt like very real pain from the Taxxon bite shot up what felt like my very real leg.

Right then I decided that this was a world I might never be able to figure out. And if I didn't stop trying to, I'd crack up. Effective immediately, my goal would be simpler: Just get out of this place alive, body and soul intact.

I tried not to let the two forms in front of me,

roughly human in outline except for a third leg and a seriously long neck, freak me too much. But it was hard.

See, each of them had only one eye, a big, internally lit thing that fixed on me like a follow spot. At the center of the eye was an iris, roughly like ours except for the faint amber and gray glow.

But you know how our pupils are in the middle of our irises? Not the case here. I was looking at pupils that orbited the iris like slow, optical satellites. These eyes studied me with all the suspicion of secret service agents at a presidential appearance. They seemed to stare right through me.

Though it's more accurate to say I stared *through* them.

Because I was looking at blue lungs that filled and deflated with speech. And two bright green hearts pumping pale yellow blood through crystal clear veins. Miles of intestines coiled tightly near a swath of faintly reddish muscle.

Their skin was as clear as glass or water. Clearer, since there was next to no distortion as I stared at the organs beneath.

Specimens a biology teacher would die for. Although on whatever planet they were from, survival of the fittest was obviously not an issue. I mean, I was staring right at a beating heart. A perfect target.

Amber Eye stepped forward and yanked me to my feet. He repeated his question. All of a sudden, the rhythm in the speech, the slightly different note that filled each word . . . The pattern. It all made sense. It clicked.

"Get-up-Orange-Suit!" he said. "What-are-you-doing-in-the-ghetto? Work-truancy-is-a-crime! Why-aren't-you-at-your-work-site?" A nearly invisible finger flicked something pinned to my chest. Then he looked up, way up, at the Chrysler Building with its Mylar sheath whipping with the wind.

There was a badge on my jumpsuit that hadn't been there before. At least, I hadn't noticed it. There was a hologram of me, and my Yeerk name written out. There were numbers corresponding to housing, work site, and work sector. Under the words "job title" was the term "Planetary Engineer."

I gaped like an idiot. These guys were some street-level security force? I worked in the Chrysler Building?

"Maybe this is the place for this mute," Silver Eye sneered. "Looks like he's had a breakdown. Can you tell us where you live, Orange Suit?" He growled patronizingly while fingering a pair of red-tinted handcuffs. "Or can't you remember?"

They could see where I lived. But I guess they just wanted me to say. I looked at my badge and tried to read the numbers upside down. "I, uh . . ."

RrrrrrrrrBoomBoom . . . RrrrrrrrrrBooooooom . . .

The earth shook and a deafening boom thundered through the street. Amber Eye spun around, then spun back and grabbed me. Dragged me with him as he moved with startling speed toward the sound of the explosion. Silver Eye followed.

"Floor eighty-eight," I said, faking an answer. "I live in the, uh, the Empire Towers." I thought that sounded pretty good.

"Don't be sarcastic, Orange Suit." He reached forward and slid the cuffs over my wrists. "You think I don't know that floors eighty-seven to ninety-two are a docking port? You're coming with us."

"Under whose authority?"

I struggled, but the cuffs were some living, organic material. The more I resisted, the tighter they squeezed.

The creatures laughed heartily, a sound like a trilling trumpet. "We're the Orff, fool. Security agents to the High Council. We're our own authority."

RrrrrrrrrBooooooooooommmmmm!

Another massive boom and cloud of dust.

The Orff turned away from me.

I made a break for it.

"Hey!"

Silver Eye grabbed for me. I wrestled free from him and shot around the corner, limping from my Taxxon bite, moving toward a billowing dust cloud. But the Orff followed me. His tripod legs moved like quicksilver. Then he was on me. We struggled as the chaos grew around us.

I heard the distant sirens of approaching hover ships. The whistled lisps of Taxxon as they burst onto the street, spilling from three-hundred-foot earthen hives built up between buildings along the block, surging like beastly commandos.

What was this? What was happening?

Could I morph? I tried to focus. Tried to think . . .

And then everything flashed a blinding yellow-white, like I was a bug inside some flashbulb. All was noiseless, but only for a second. Then —

BOOM.

BOOM.

BOOM!

The pavement heaved and thumped as deafening pressure waves threw everyone in the street to the ground. All down the block, entire building fronts were instantly reduced to lethal waterfalls of shattering glass and stone.

I raised my head toward what appeared to be

the source of the explosion. A tremendous sky-scraper, towering hundreds of feet, a fireball at its base, teetered hesitatingly, like a circus performer on a tightrope.

My mouth opened in disbelief as the building's graceful, tentative sway gave way to decisive instability. As the lowest ten or twenty stories disintegrated in a cloud of dust.

Then the entire structure sailed toward Earth. Faster . . . faster . . . toppling in a single rigid section. Falling . . . falling . . . then —

A thunderous concussion as the building ruptured and broke in two, missing the Chrysler Building by what seemed like a hair.

Concussion after concussion battered the Manhattan bedrock. I should have taken the chance to disappear.

But it was all I could do to crawl to a doorway and lie there, as a choking cloud of white dust engulfed me and a spattering of small debris rained down from the sky.

Then heavier particles, chunks of steel and concrete, were pummeling the street. And then everything went black.

CHAPTER 11

Sirens blared. A splitting pain numbed my head.

I opened my eyes to piles of rubble. Spewing geysers from burst watermains. Fires crackling, ripping through entire buildings. Hundreds of patrol ships on the scene. Taxxons savagely herding the injured into transports, satisfying their raging hunger by disposing of the dead right there and then.

The Orff were gone. The cuffs, somehow, vanished. Apparently, when you're in Yeerk Land and you hear sirens and they're coming to get you, you don't wait around. You move.

I sprinted from the doorway.

"Ahhrgh!"

55

And slammed smack into a purple suit. Before I could regain balance, I was looking down the barrel of a handheld Dracon.

Yeerk Land definitely had it in for me.

I looked past the barrel, past the arm. Into the eyes of a dark female figure covered head-to-foot in dust. Blood dripped from even features. As our eyes met, her expression changed. It flashed from ruthless hatred to a mysterious mix of confusion, disbelief, tenderness, and anger.

My chest heaved involuntarily because this woman . . .

This woman . . . my memory . . .

"Ah!"

Without warning she shoved me out of the way.

TSEEEW!

Whumph.

Taxxon guts spilled onto the pavement as the bloated worm, teeth bared, skidded to a halt just shy of my legs. Three seconds more and my butt would have been nothing more than a pleasant Taxxon aftertaste.

The woman darted ahead. I sprinted after her. She'd saved my life.

But it was for more than that that I followed.

With the agility of a triathlete, she scampered

down a narrow alley mounded with discarded remnants of human society. A broken piano. Couch carcasses. Some rusting motorcycles. All of it covered over now in a fresh mountain of concrete, rebar, and fragments of still-steaming sheet metal.

I called to her. "Hey, wait." She paused and turned back.

I rushed eagerly forward and her face turned strange again like she was searching her mind, searching . . .

TSEEEW!

"Hey! What the . . ."

She'd fired at me, igniting the air over my head. Then she disappeared through a large metal door opening off the alley, a side entrance to a tall brick building.

Was that a warning shot? Or just bad aim?

A gang of Taxxons flowed down the alley and followed her inside. I picked up a piece of metal and swung it like a thug, trying to show I was ready to fight. They snarled, but amazingly, they ran right by.

One thing was clear. They were after the woman.

I flung open the thick metal door and ran into the mottled darkness. Light filtered through a partially blown off roof and illuminated velvety curtains, a stage, an orchestra pit — a vast space lined with rows of seats and tiers of balconies. I moved down the carpeted aisle, hoisted myself onto the stage littered with broken flats.

TSEEEW! TSEEEW!

Dracon fire lit the air. A 500-pound mass of Taxxon meat fell from the grid, whistling past a wall of ropes and rigging.

WHUMP.

It shook the floor. An exploded balloon. And boy, did it stink.

The woman streaked behind a drop painted with a scenic country setting. There was a red barn and green pasture. Horses and farm animals grazed in the background.

But no sooner had she disappeared than . . .

TSEEEW!

She burned a Dracon hole in the faded canvas landscape and vaulted through. Chasing after her were three of the fastest Taxxons I'd ever seen. She stumbled, running backward, firing her weapon again and again. But the discharges grew weaker and weaker, pathetic slaps in the face to the hulking Taxxons.

And I was weaponless!

I looked up at row upon row of heavy lights. I wondered . . .

I ran into the wings, where the myriad ropes converge in neat rows anchored by stacks of steel weights.

I threw open the latch that fixed a rope to its stack of anchors.

Whooooosh!

An ethereal cloth backdrop came billowing down, deftly covering the predators and the prey below.

Not happening.

The Taxxons continued to surge forward until at last, the woman's faulty weapon wouldn't fire anymore. She hurled it at the closest Taxxon, but it was like a toy in his mouth. It was swallowed up without hesitation.

I frantically disconnected rope after rope. The racing whine of pulleys filled my ears as a whole batten of heavy stage lights came crashing to the floor. And then another. And another.

I let myself look. Three bloated Taxxons were pinned to the floor, writhing. Still caught under the delicate scrim net.

I ran to the woman. Her arm was being crushed by a now-limp Taxxon. Her body was washed in a puddle of vile drool. She flinched as I neared her, still ready to fight.

I bent low and freed her arm. She finally seemed to understand that I wasn't going to hurt her.

Our eyes met.

"Cassie."

I wanted to hug her. Tell her everything was

okay. That she was brave. That we would make it out alive.

But her eyes were like a wall or a mask. I searched them for the peace and sensitivity they used to hold.

Neither was there.

Her lips curled into a fake smile, a very un-Cassie-like look. And she finally spoke.

"So. You're not dead."

CHAPTER 12

I answered with a smile, the kind of look I'd have given her if we were back in the world I knew.

"This city's been doing all it can to kill me. But no, I'm not dead. I've been alone. Where are the others? How . . . how did you get here?"

She didn't answer, but swung her legs over the stage apron, heaved a sigh, and dropped into the orchestra pit. I followed her down, where she stooped in a corner and uncovered a stashed case.

"Cassie, what's going on?" It wasn't like her to ignore me. She didn't even look up. "I got into bed, just last night, I think," I continued. "I was at home, living with my family. We'd just come back from our last messed-up mission. Remem-

61

ber? I wake up this morning and I'm freakin' twenty-five years old. With a beard and no memory of the decade in between. Is this Crayak? The Ellimist?"

"I haven't thought of those names in years," she said. Her tone was not nostalgic. She was rummaging through the case, I guessed for bandages to fix a splint to her arm. The case was filled with first-aid supplies, five or six handheld Dracons, another purple suit, emergency food rations, and . . .

She turned her head just in time to see my eyes widen.

Spools of blast cord. Blocks of plastic explosives. Detonators. Dynamite. A crazy mix of low- and high-tech destructive potential.

"I take it you're not with the EF?" she said.

I shook my head.

"The Evolutionist Front. The Yeerk rebel group? You know, the so-called Insurrectionists, dedicated to turning away from parasitism and toward the use of artificially created symbiotes?"

She shoved a Dracon into my hand and took two for herself. And then I glimpsed an emergency Kandrona particle emitter as she closed the case.

"You're a Controller?"

She laughed. "What else would I be? My Yeerk's name is Niss. We're in the EF together. We cooperate to fight the Council. I led the team responsible for the blast this morning. That's why the Taxxons like me so much. The damage will set them back, even though we didn't hit the . . ."

"What!" An uncontrollable wave of nausea knotted my chest. It was like hearing my dad confess to being a drug pusher or a murderer. It was an impossibility. "Cassie, what are you saying? You engineered a blast that must have killed hundreds of refugees, the very people the EF is trying to help? That makes you a terrorist! How can you possibly justify that?"

"In a war, Jake, anything is justified." She spoke with an unnerving confidence. "I'm not a kid anymore. I'm not concerned with the nonsense I used to be."

"Like life and peace? You think that's nonsense now! Don't you remember our last mission — the Ragsin Building battle? The comedown? You needed to talk when we got out and I turned you away. Just didn't want to deal with it. I was an idiot that night, Cassie. You were on target with your doubts, just like you always were. You have to realize that."

She laughed dismissively. "You're talking about a different lifetime, Jake. There were so many missions back then. All just a pitiful blur of youthful idealism. You don't get it, do you? I'm saying that I finally understand war."

The way she was speaking, the way she was sort of talking down to me, made me feel like I was about as important to her as a screw in the stage floor.

Was there really no connection between us? Was my friend so changed?

"The Taxxons own the subway," I said. "The Orff rule the streets. Cassie, if you look around, it's obvious that somehow we lost our chance to win this war."

"The war is not lost!" she hissed. Her eyes were on fire. She looked ready to attack me.

But then her eyes moved to the badge on my chest and all at once her anger vanished. Her face relaxed, then brightened. Her expression changed so quickly it was frightening.

CHAPTER 13

"You're a planetary engineer? Working on the Chrysler Building project!" Suddenly, I was the most interesting thing in the theater. I didn't know what to say. She moved toward me. Her uninjured arm gripped my arm. Her voice was intense, almost obsessed.

"Jake, the Yeerks want the moon. They want to make it a small, Kandrona-radiating sun. If they succeed, it means an Earth bathed in Kandrona rays for the rest of eternity! It'll be something the EF could never touch and never disable. No one could."

I felt like a customer subjected to an intricate and manipulative sales pitch. The deal-maker was just around the corner, I could feel it. And I knew it somehow involved me.

"Your job brings you closer to the moon-ray technology than anyone in the EF. You know that shell over the Chrysler Building? The Yeerks have been working under there for months, fine-tuning the energy beam that will ignite the moon. The targeting has to be precise. Absolutely precise. The Yeerks need the beam to fire exactly the way you and your team have calculated, or else . . ."

She was animated. Her eyes glistened as she stood before me. There was the spark I knew. Only it wasn't love of people or animals that put it there. It was thoughts of sabotage, terrorism, strategy.

And now she was drawing me into it, too.

I brought my fingers to the badge her eyes still fixed on. I yanked it off, breaking her trance.

"Tell me right now! How did we get here? Where are the others? How were you captured? Is this even real?"

Her enthusiasm settled. The fake smile re-appeared. She didn't want to answer my questions, but if she wanted my help, she had to.

"If you really don't remember, I'll tell you," she said. "You won't like the answer." She laughed again a little. Less ruthless, more rueful, she looked me in the eyes. "How was I captured? I was betrayed, Jake. By you."

My heart stopped.

"Me!"

"Well, you were a Controller by then, of course. You can thank Tom for that."

"My brother?"

She nodded. "The Yeerk in Tom's head finally put it all together. Clues, maybe. Carelessness. I don't know. But he suspected you of being an 'Andalite bandit' and then one night, he was sure. He planned his attack so well that when it came, you didn't stand a chance."

She continued. "You, Marco, and Ax were taken immediately, in my barn. Rachel was killed outright. They caught me the next day. Only Tobias escaped."

A tightness constricted my throat. Rachel dead?! There was a time when I'd encouraged her recklessness. I'd put her, more than any of the others, in dangerous spots. And Tobias? With a hawk's life span, he'd be dead by now.

Cassie told me all of this matter-of-factly, like I should know the story. Like I should have known that this, all of it, was because of me . . .

"Move!"

TSEEEW!

The black metal music stands in front of me vaporized.

"Get down!"

TSEEEW!

Cassie returned fire, striking the Taxxon. He keeled over, falling forward, falling right over the rail above the orchestra pit! Flailing fifteen feet to the floor. Crash! Writhing in agony at our feet.

He was badly wounded, but he'd live. Maybe Cassie'd shot him in the hind quarters on purpose, so he'd survive. All we had to do was run.

I opened the access door to the crawlspace under the stage.

"Cassie, come on!" She ducked in. I followed.

But then she stopped. She turned. She aimed right past me, back through the door.

TSEEEW!

A second hole sizzled through the Taxxon's vital organs, coldly finishing him off.

I looked at Cassie, searched her for an answer, tried to understand eyes ablaze with ruthlessness.

"They're just dogs," she said. "The Orffs' unofficial police squad let loose to catch us socalled terrorists. The Orff don't mind too much if Taxxon hunger gets out of control and they eat us instead of bringing us to the station. An eye for an eye, I say."

I wondered if maybe this was Niss talking. The Yeerk, and not Cassie.

"Come on!" she yelled.

I followed her.

CHAPTER 14

We burst into the street. Ran away from the sound of sirens and hover ships and a still-chaotic crime scene.

Every hundred yards, Cassie turned back to return fire. The Taxxons finally fell off and we stopped at a smashed-up storefront. An old newsstand.

Sweating and panting, I glanced at the racks. The sunburned, wind-tattered cover of an old *Sports Illustrated* caught my eye. I picked it up.

"My dad . . ." I said with surprise. "He just got this issue in the mail!" Cassie looked at the date.

"Yeah," she said flatly, "it's been about ten years. The Yeerk conquest concluded in a matter

69

of weeks after we were captured. Turns out we were more than a thorn in the side of the Empire. We'd actually started to shift the balance."

And then I'd blown it.

I'd gotten careless and cocky and ruthless myself. I'd been too ready to use the others, especially Rachel.

"The others," I said. "Where are they now?"

Cassie paused next to a ratty pile of romance novels. "Ax became a high-ranking Controller. From what I heard, he was the key player in the Yeerk attack on his home world. The Andalite planet was decimated. Millions died. Tens of thousands of Andalites were taken. EF leadership thinks there are some still free in deep space, but I can't imagine . . . "

I sank to the floor beside a stack of yellowed *New York Times* dated three weeks from the night I fell into bed in spandex bike shorts.

"Tobias became a leader of sorts. Anti-Yeerk."

"Does he — did he — know about Rachel?"

"Yes. As for Marco." Her voice turned colder. "Marco's Visser Two now, in charge of Earth. He's done things . . . terrible things."

This wasn't real. I couldn't be hearing this. I didn't believe it.

"The Visser Three you remember was made head of the Council. The supreme Yeerk leader. Emperor."

No. Cassie's Yeerk was feeding me lies. She was wearing me down. She knew . . . she knew from Cassie's memory what would get to me, what could make me snap.

But I wouldn't snap! I wasn't crazy. My friends weren't . . . No. My friends . . . No!

Suddenly, I was running down an empty street. I didn't care that I had nowhere to go. I'd just keep running and running until I collapsed. "Free or die," I repeated to myself. "Free or die!"

"Free or . . . "

"Stop it!"

Cassie cut in front of me and pushed me against the wall. Only then did I feel my face streaked with tears. My eyes blurred. My chest heaving.

"It was good luck that I met you, Jake. The job you have as planetary engineer is an incredible chance for the EF." Cassie was intense and obsessed again. "The controlled burn of the moon the Empire is planning? We need to make it uncontrolled. The perfect targeting of the energy beam? We need it to be off. Exploding the moon will shower the earth with debris. It will knock out satellites, destroy spacecraft, disrupt the entire Yeerk social structure. It will create an opening for attack by the EF. Jake, do you hear me? It will be the opening the EF and free humans have been waiting for."

71

Two of her words struck my ears like bells. "Free humans?"

"Yes. Small groups still survive in the countryside. Hunted groups of fugitives."

"So, there's hope?"

"I told you the war wasn't lost. But it will be. All hope will be erased if this energy beam fires as the Yeerks want it to. Go to work." She knew I'd help her. She knew she was my leader now. "Live the life your badge describes. Watch, listen, get information, scope things out. But don't act until I contact you. I'll send someone who works with me to give you instructions. We'll need a code word."

Reluctantly, I clipped my badge back onto my jumpsuit. "How about 'peace'?" I said with a weak smile.

Cassie looked at me like I was a naive two-year-old. She reached out and touched my face tenderly. And for an instant, one sweet instant, the mask of hardness lifted. The girl I'd loved was looking back at me.

But she was gone as quickly as she'd come.

"It's too late for peace, Jake. All that's left now is to drive the invaders away by force. Make Earth too dangerous for them. How about a different code word? How about . . . 'Animorphs'?"

I agreed and she was gone, leaving me with a

Dracon beam in my hand and emptiness in my heart.

Was I on her side? I thought I wanted to be. She'd assumed I would be.

But she was so changed. Driven. Obsessed. Ultrafocused. She'd become a cog in the war machine. But then, who here wasn't?

Was I a pawn in her mind? A mere tool?

I knew the answer.

But I didn't care.

It might help me save her.

CHAPTER 15

I boarded a shuttle that dropped me on an empty docking pad, cantilevered off the face of the building two hundred feet above the street. The Chrysler Building's Mylar wrap gleamed reddish-brown in the city's frightening glow.

A powerful gust slapped me off balance and ripped at my hair as I stepped toward a heavy steel panel.

The panel began to rise.

How would I save our moon from transfiguration, from becoming a beacon of Yeerk strength, an irreversible enemy triumph? How could I obliterate the chance that Kandrona would forever taint Earth's surface with its malignant rays?

If only I had clear-cut instructions, like: Infiltrate enemy science headquarters, corrupt the latest state-of-the-art Yeerk technology, blow up the moon. Hey, that even sounded vaguely familiar. We'd done stuff like that before, right? No problem.

But it wasn't that simple. She said I had to wait.

Wait for orders from a Cassie I didn't even know! Why was I letting it happen? No Animorph would ever take orders from a Yeerk. Hadn't I made that a ground rule?

I stepped across the threshold. Second-guessing my decision to help Cassie. And third-guessing it, and fourth-guessing it.

The panel shut behind me, sealing out the immutable hum I'd come to know meant Yeerk business as usual. Small, triangular lights reddened the floor, pointing me toward a nearby gravity lift. With all the false confidence I could muster I entered the clear, semicircular enclosure, hovering in the air just outside the Mylar sheath. There were a half-dozen other riders. Two humans, an Andalite, and some pinkish creatures I'd never seen before.

<Figured you had abandoned us for the home world,> the Andalite teased.

"Had to visit the clinic. Problems with my host. He has a rebellious history."

"I hear you, man," said a tall human male.

"My host used to work for the ACLU and he just won't shut up about how I'm infringing on his rights. I don't want to worry you, but the pills don't really work."

The lift rushed upward with unsettling acceleration. I put a hand on the wall for balance and looked out over the corridor of death and wreckage carved by the explosion. The collapsed skyscraper still smoked and cindered.

<They seem to grow stronger every day,> the Andalite commented. He didn't say who "they" were, but I knew he meant the EF. His voice was calm enough, the way you'd expect a member of the ruling class to sound when speaking of the oppressed. But his tone revealed more. Today's explosion marked a turning point. In the mind of this Andalite-Controller, the EF had just crossed the line from nuisance to threat.

"You're just in time for this afternoon's group efficiency workshop," piped up another of the humans. "Peer Communication Skills — Conquest through Companionship."

"Never miss one," I stated positively.

The lift doors opened onto a vast room. A sea of short, shiny, stainless steel cubicles shone under glaring lights. I followed the taller human into a large open area with metal stools, most already occupied. A holographic short film played at the front of the room. It depicted an Andalite-

Controller passing the cubicle of a Hork-Bajir-Controller.

<May the Kandrona shine and strengthen you,> the Andalite said. The Hork-Bajir didn't respond, just kept working.

The holo paused at that frame and a female Andalite at the front of the room asked the assembled group, <What was missing from that interaction that could have facilitated team compatibility?>

That's a tough one, lady, I thought. *But I'll go out on a limb here and guess that it's free* will.

I turned on my heels and wound through the paths between cubicle walls. I had no idea where I was going, but I pretended I did. Almost everyone smiled as I passed. One guy even slapped my back and said, "Hey, Essak. Ready for the big night?"

The big night. What was that about? The guy in the hovercraft had asked me about a launch.

Were the Yeerks firing this moon ray tonight?!

Find your desk, Jake. I looked at my badge. Sector 5-682. The cubicles had number plates: 679, 680, 681.

I stood over the computer monitor assigned to me. A model of the Chrysler Building spire rotated and twisted its way across the screen. It was framed by strings of numbers that changed as the model turned.

It was just like that dream where you show up for the final exam in some class, and it suddenly

77

hits you that you haven't studied at all. In fact, you haven't been to the class at all and now you have to pass the test.

I looked around. Everyone else had silver probes hung on their ears. There was one on my desk. It looked like a tape dispenser, but I picked it off the console and fit it to my ear. Looked at the monitor. And suddenly . . .

Whoa! The 3-D model flashed! The image was uncontrollable. Unstoppable! My brain was panicking, racing. I tried to mask the monitor from view so that my cubicle neighbors wouldn't sound the impostor alarm.

Then, I realized . . .

I controlled the movement. The screen reflected whatever command my mind issued. Under other circumstances, this would have been extremely cool. *Slow,* I ordered, *easy.* My mind relaxed and so did the images. I made the screen flip through pictures at a normal speed.

I was just about to breathe a sigh of relief when I felt eyes staring at me. I looked up.

There was a communal workstation directly in front of my cubicle. I'd passed through it on my way. Noticed focused, hardworking aliens of various species, studying their own screens, consulting other screens.

Now, they'd stopped working.

"Boss?" a Hork-Bajir huskily. "You okay, boss?"

78

Oh, my God. These guys were working for me and they'd seen my screen wig out! Did they know I was a phony, a fake, an infiltrator? Could they tell?

I moved to shuffle papers on my desk, to look occupied and cover up my ignorance, but there weren't any papers to shuffle. "Yup," I said casually. I tinkered with my earpiece and frowned down at my screen, seriouslike. "I was just, you know, giving the old mind a rest."

After a few seconds, I glanced back at the communal workstation, hoping my crew had returned to business and forgotten everything they'd just seen me do.

But when I looked at my crew, I saw . . . my crew . . .

CHAPTER 16

Seats just moments ago occupied by busy Controllers — healthy, breathing, living Controllers — now held . . .

I blinked just to make sure.

Oh, yeah.

The seats held the raw, bloody, dismembered bodies of enemies I had faced in battle. My past was staring back at me.

You have to understand that I really didn't think what I was seeing was real. And yet, under the harsh fluorescent lights, there was no mistaking that the corpses were there.

A Hork-Bajir corpse rose out of a chair. His mauled body had been ripped apart by the claws of my tiger morph. How could he stand?! He wasn't even breathing! His muscles were decomposing! And yet he staggered out from behind the console and started toward me.

He stretched his arm forward, extended his wrist blade and reached . . . reached for me! A growling rumbled in a voice box that wasn't there. Tiger jaws had ripped it out.

I turned to run. I was crazy. I was nuts!

Total insanity was twisting my brain!

But when I tried to move, my path was blocked by a Leeran's stocky form, its pebbly, slimy skin run dry.

"Ahh!" Its webbed feet had been severed by a shark's teeth. My shark morph's teeth. Only thin, fibrous ligaments kept the feet moving with the body. The large, luminous, Leeran eyes were lifeless.

And yet he shuffled toward me, and I felt him say my name.

Jake, he chanted. *Jake, Jake, Jake, Jake, Jake.*

I stiffened and backed into my cubicle. I could smell them now. Their decay and rot. Death, pressing nearer and nearer!

Behind the Hork-Bajir, a Taxxon's jelly eyes gaped and a three-foot tongue dangled limp from its open mouth. A tiger slash had flayed it from neck to belly. Its innards oozed. Flies swarmed at the opening. Maggots churned in the wound. Lobsterlike Taxxon claws clacked like castanets as it strained and reached for me.

Jake, Jake, Jake, Jake.

The chanting continued. The smells, the growling, the buzzing flies, the blood . . .

"No," I breathed. It's a vision. This is your past . . . haunting you . . . This isn't real!

Not real!

I needed to climb over the cubicle wall. They were coming!

Jake, Jake, Jake, Jake.

I put a hand on the partition and tried to pull myself over it, but I had no strength.

A rat appeared between the corpses' slow-moving feet. Running blindly, frantically. Bumping into dismembered alien parts. Recoiling, then starting out again. I knew it was David. The kid we turned into an Animorph. The kid who betrayed us. One bad decision after another. Trapped and helpless because of me . . .

Corpses had crowded into my cubicle! The Leeran's tentacles brushed my arm!

"No!"

The Taxxon's claws closed over my fingers!

A raw, blood-dipped Hork-Bajir claw pressed against my cheek.

I closed my eyes. My heart pounded.

82

The rat scampered up my leg and sank its teeth into my skin.

"Nooo!"

The bodies of the enemies I'd destroyed . . .

"No, No, NOOOOO!"

"KEEEEEEEE-row!"

I opened my eyes and the cubicle had disappeared. I was tumbling through the air, spinning, plummeting out of control! I was in wild free fall next to a Howler.

"KEEEEEE-row!"

Another mind-splitting cry! The planet floor was racing up! The Howler was clawing the air, screaming in rage. Screaming! Because I'd led him off the ledge.

Rat teeth sliced my skin. Webbed fingers slapped at my face. A Taxxon tongue covered me with spit. Hork-Bajir blades began to slice . . .

The ground, racing up!

"KEEEEEEEE-row!"

I couldn't take anymore. Too much! Too much!

"AHH! AHH! AHH!" I screamed and screamed and screamed.

Then, instantly, all went silent.

I gasped and jumped up from where I lay, sweating and cowering against the cool cubicle wall.

Confused, out of my mind, I stared ahead.

"Boss?"

I jerked my head toward the communal work-station. Normal Controllers sat behind the console, a Hork-Bajir and a Taxxon among them.

They looked at me in alarmed disbelief.

I felt like I always did when I woke from a nightmare. Startled, a little embarrassed, but mostly just grateful that even this reality was less than the terror of the dream.

There was a bustling down the hall.

Orff and Hork-Bajir steamed through the maze of cubicles. Security was heading straight for me.

Leading them, storming fast and angrily, was a stone-faced human, tall and sturdily built. I felt I should know this person.

There was something familiar . . .

"Get him!" he roared. The guards moved as one.

It couldn't be true. Yet it was true. This wasn't another nightmare vision. It was real!

The man who was ordering a security force to apprehend me was the man who'd played catch with me as a child, who'd taught me how to swim. The man who had changed my diapers.

My friend. My role model.

My father.

CHAPTER 17

Magically clear, steel-strong Orff fingers clutched my arms as my father approached. He looked just as I remembered him. Salt-and-pepper hair receding slightly. A vertical wrinkle forged above his nose. He hadn't aged a day. How was that possible?

"Dad . . ."

His face showed no response as his eyes tracked, sifting his memory.

"That's right. Once upon a time, you were my host's son. This is quite a coincidence in a city so big."

My thoughts exactly.

It was a weird and unlikely coincidence. As an isolated event, maybe. I'm out of commission for ten years and when I tune in again, my dad's there waiting to arrest me. Sure.

But combined with bumping into Cassie? With sighting Tobias? With learning that it was my carelessness that led to Rachel's death?

Too much convergence. Too many life lines intersecting.

There had to be some other current at work here.

"You were late for work," the Yeerk in my father's head accused. "Late and in the vicinity of the explosion. You will be interrogated."

The Orff squeezed my arms, nearly cutting off the blood flow.

This is a dream, I thought again. *Or maybe I have a fever. I'll wake up in a cold sweat, back in my room, back with a chance for victory . . .*

"Move him!"

The guards pulled me forward. I leaned back.

Wake up, I screamed silently. *Wake up!*

I wanted it to be a dream. Willed it to be a fevered dream.

The Orffs' blue lungs filled and collapsed, filled and collapsed. Their hearts contracted. Their blood coursed.

I rammed an elbow into a lung.

No response!

A flash of insight. What if their organs, those blatant, exposed, vulnerable organs, were decoys? By all biological laws, they should be. They could be drawing attention away from the body sections that mattered.

With a sweep of my leg I knocked one to the floor. He released my arm and I packed the hardest punch I've ever thrown at the clearest part of the other Orff's chest. Just below the head, but above the heart. A section clear as air.

The sea-green glow in his eye faltered and flickered out. He moaned and fell, an unconscious heap. My father's face flashed alarm.

"Take him!"

Two Hork-Bajir lunged. I turned and ran for the gravity lift, but six more Hork-Bajir came running from that direction. Roping me in! Closing off escape!

I was blocked. Surrounded. Helpless!

Unless . . .

I focused.

And the impossible began to happen.

Bands of color, stripes of orange and black inked my skin. Then fur erupted. Tiger muscles bulged, ripping my suit at its seams. My teeth enlarged and sharpened, becoming rows of pointed spears.

I was still able to morph.

The Yeerk force stared in horror, incredulous.

"He's not Andalite! It's impossible!"

Not so, boys.

I fell forward onto all fours and lunged. Slashed a Hork-Bajir leg. Rip! Slash! Rip!

Four were down. I turned on my father. He reached for the Dracon holstered on his hip.

His hand was on it. His eyes were on me.

One leap and I'd have him. One leap, and I could take him out.

My dad.

He lifted the beam from his belt. Started to bring it up.

One leap . . .

Take down my father?

WHAM!

From behind! A brutal blow. My head exploded. My legs, crumpling beneath me. And my vision . . .

Red, then black.

CHAPTER 18

Slowly, very slowly, unconsciousness gave way to the numb daze of waking up.

My limbs were heavy. Utter exhaustion made me happy to be lying down. *Don't move. Don't even open your eyes. Back to sleep. Yeah . . . go back to sleep, Jake.*

Then suddenly, I remembered.

Panic knotted my stomach. I was back in human form!

How did I demorph?

Hideous red light reflected off a cool, smooth floor. It burned my eyes. Bare, seamless walls. A large room. And I was sprawled near the exit. A door frame with no door. I could go . . .

I staggered to my feet, scanned the hall outside for guards. No one. This was it. My lucky break. I rushed forward.

Kzzzzt!

It was like being slapped down by a steel plate. My face, knees, and fists had struck an invisible, electrified force. I raised my head, not sure of what had happened, anticipating a second strike.

Nothing. Just the opening, still crackling from impact.

I struggled to raise my limp body.

"Still putting up the big fight?" It was a deep, chiding voice. "After all these years?"

I looked up. A broad, dark man paused in the doorway, then strode through the energy barrier. He was flanked by six Hork-Bajir and four heavily armed Orff. The Hork-Bajir fell off and took up locations by the entrance. The Orff kept their positions on either side of this person, who was clearly in charge.

He spoke.

"When they told me it was you, I didn't believe it. I thought you'd been disposed of at the beginning. My host's old comrade in arms. The former leader of that pathetic little gang, the Animorphs."

The face was adult. Mid-twenties, like mine. Unmistakable anywhere, despite all that had changed. Despite the deep, angular battle scars that scored it.

I knew that face.

That cocky confidence. That swagger.

"Marco?"

"Just the parts of his mind I find useful," came the reply. A voice at once familiar and alien.

"Not you, too, man."

"Your old friend Marco's serving the Empire now, if that's what you mean. He finally understands how much better things can be when we all work together. One big happy family. Tell your old buddy, Marco."

An odd expression contorted the man's face. A face so shocked to find it could speak, that the mouth could barely form words.

There was stuttering. A long attempt to utter something.

"N-n-n . . . o."

And then the mouth stopped abruptly, turning once again cold and hard. The Yeerk cut in. The Yeerk who'd stolen my best friend's mind and made him a slave.

"What he means is that no one could be happier."

"Marco would die before he'd choose to help you."

"Evolutionist-Front nonsense. Everyone wants to help the Yeerks. It's the informed choice, the 'in' thing to do. Life's cool when you share your head."

This Yeerk was trying hard to tap Marco's humor, but it wasn't working.

"You'll want to join us, too. We've already got a new Yeerk lined up for you. Someone more cooperative with the Empire. He'll help you think things through, help that anarchic brain of yours find peace. But first we've got some business to take care of."

A new Yeerk? So he, too, thought I was already a Controller?

I knew I wasn't. I knew it!

And yet when everybody thinks you're something you're not, when everyone tells you again and again who and what you are, it's hard not to wonder, way in the back of your mind, if they aren't somehow right.

CHAPTER 19

"You were spotted on the street near the scene of the explosion. You were off duty without authorization. Then I hear you're hanging with Gotham's most wanted. I have to say it was that particular piece of evidence that sealed your fate." A familiar smirk lit up the altered face. "Old Jake's a terrorist."

"I don't know anything about the explosion. I was just on my way to work."

"I anticipated you'd try to resist."

Marco snapped his fingers and a Hork-Bajir swiftly disabled the energy barrier. Two Orff marched in, carrying Cassie. Her feet and hands were bound with living handcuffs. They handled her roughly, ignoring her broken arm.

Despite her injury, Cassie fought them like a madwoman. She spat in the big Cyclopean eye of an Orff. The orbiting pupil turned from bright yellow to beet-red. He threw her to the floor at Marco's feet.

"Terrorist or not," Marco said to me, "when you see what I can do to Cassie, you'll do as I say."

Cassie started to crawl away, but the Orff grabbed her again and dragged her to a corner of the room. They fastened her cuffs to brackets on the wall.

"I want to meet those people clever enough to bring down a building in the center of town, right under our noses," Marco said, his calm unnerving. "I'd like you to introduce me to that group of individuals. If you're willing, Jake, I think we might be able to keep things friendly."

No. I was going to free Cassie. She needed help.

I was about to morph to tiger when she caught my eye. Her expression held me back. Its meaning was clear. *Hold your ground, Jake,* her eyes said. *Tell him nothing. Keep your cool. If you try to free me, you'll tell him too much.*

So I didn't morph. Instead I turned to Marco and said, "I told you, I don't know anything about any group."

Immediately, led in by two more Orff, came a

gigantic Taxxon on a leash. Each Orff carried a long pointed pole with which they jabbed at the Taxxon, keeping it at bay.

Marco snickered. "This fellow's been brought straight over from the Taxxon home world where he made quite a name for himself. He ate his entire hive. Mother? Uh-huh. Father? Yep. Siblings? Children? Cousins? Oh, yeah. We tried infesting him, but it became obvious that he's more effective at what he does when his natural inclinations are left unchecked."

The Taxxon pulled violently, choking on his leash, oblivious to everything but the search for flesh. Hundreds of legs scrambled. The Orff could barely hold him back.

Cassie squirmed, struggling to break free. I thought she would pull her arms out of their sockets. I couldn't watch.

"Help us infiltrate the EF," Marco propositioned smoothly, "and her life will be spared. Tell me all you know and . . ."

"Tell him nothing!" Cassie snarled. "I'd sooner die a thousand Taxxon-deaths than aid the Empire."

She meant it. No childish uncertainty lingered in her voice. No naive hopes. She was pure warrior, calculating as any visser.

But when I looked at her face, even though it was ten years older than in my memory, I saw only the Cassie I once knew, the Cassie I once cared for.

She saw my mind working.

"No, Jake!" she yelled.

"Decide now or it's over for the girl. You won't have a second chance."

I looked from Cassie to Marco, and didn't even hesitate.

"I'll tell you whatever you want."

"No!" Cassie shrieked, bucking and kicking. Marco signaled. An Orff clamped see-through fingers over Cassie's mouth.

"This makes a new record for breaking a terrorist." Marco smiled and fell into a chair. "It's things like this that get you noticed by the Council. They knew what they were doing when they made me Visser Three."

Visser Three?

"Cassie said you were Visser Two."

"I am."

"But you just said . . . you said three, not two."

Marco's grin broadened.

That was a slip. Proof that this couldn't be real!

"It's all just a dream, isn't it?" I said excitedly.

Marco laughed. "Dream? Reality? Can you tell

the difference? Are you so sure there even is a difference? Pain is pain. Fear is fear. If I order this Taxxon to eat you now you'll feel agony beyond imagining. Call it a dream if you want, but it'll be real enough."

I looked at Cassie, still screaming muffled syllables through the Orff's fingers.

I looked at the Taxxon. He saw me and jerked his head. Drool flew from his mouth. Struck my hand.

"You'll do just as I say. Exactly as I say, or this Taxxon scarfs Cassie down in a New York minute. Get it?"

I got it.

"Start talking."

"Okay," I said nervously. "I'm waiting for further contact from the EF. They're planning another attack. Worse than the one today," I added, though I would not mention the moon-ray plan. "I don't have details yet. I get them from my next contact. I'll cooperate. I'll do whatever you want. Just don't hurt her."

"Her?" Marco said, rising from his chair, moving toward Cassie. "Why would we have to harm her?" His voice was calm, confident. "She'll give us the names of the other EF terrorists. She'll give us their locations. She'll help us catch them, help us reinfest them. Relax, Jake. I'm sure . . ."

Cassie head-butted the Orff. His fingers fell away from her mouth. She coughed, back deep in her throat, and —

Dead center. Marco's right eye. She lodged the perfect loogie.

No one spoke.

Marco reached out and gripped her hair. Bent her head back. Pulled so hard she squinted. Then he let go of her, rubbed the spit out of his eye, and turned to me.

"Go back to work, Jake. Essak. Wait for the EF to contact you. Go with them. Do as they say. We'll be watching."

The room began to spin.

"No matter which way you turn, we'll know. We'll be there. Don't try to deceive us."

I grabbed the table for support. But the room just kept spinning. And spinning . . .

"We'll be watching." Marco's voice was faint now. "Every step you take, Jake. Buddy . . ."

CHAPTER 20

Awake. Somehow, back at my work console.

Controllers all over the office began quietly standing up, leaving their cubicles, systematically filing out of the big room toward the gravity-lift doors.

My computer was blank. No more rotating Chrysler Building model. Glowing numerals glared 6:36. The workday was over. My crew was already gone, which was lucky, because I would have had a lot of explaining to do.

Dreams within nightmares within hallucinations within visions. It was debilitating!

Play along. Get up and follow.

We'll be watching . . .

Marco's voice still vibrated in my ears.

I picked up the mug on my desk that had somehow appeared and took a swig of cold coffee. I bit into a half-eaten jelly donut. It moved down my esophagus like a wad of wet paper towel.

I stood up and followed the last Controller onto the gravity lift. It plummeted several floors and opened onto a long, yellow hallway. Pulsating triangles pointed the way to an enclosed bridge. A catwalk, running from skyscraper to skyscraper over dingy streets hundreds of feet below.

I heard music. A thumping bass filled the air. I quickened my step. Inviting smells. Food smells.

I followed the music and aromas to a huge carpeted room, like a banquet hall. Blue and red lights flashed and spun in the darkness. Long tables lined the walls and framed a dance floor. Orff lifted crystal mugs of green brew into the air, chanted something incomprehensible, downed the liquid, and slammed the mugs to the table. At the far end, a ring of Taxxons stuffed pot pie after pot pie into their mouths, cheered on by Hork-Bajir.

But much of the crowd was human. Evidently the Yeerks understood the human need for leisure time. And for junk food.

Tacos, hamburgers, chicken strips, cheese sticks, buffalo wings. Bowls of chips piled three feet high. No broccoli in sight. My mother would not be happy. I was in heaven. Nightmare or not, it was real enough that I felt hunger. Hunger so strong I felt I'd been adrift for a month in the raging Pacific with nothing to sustain me but rainwater.

I heaped a plate with tacos and pizza and edged toward the drink bar.

WHOOF!

A Hork-Bajir slammed me against the wall, knocking my plate to the floor.

I moved to strike. He blocked my arm.

"Don't struggle," he said quietly. "I'm a friend."

I looked him over. Savage blades. Bandana strips tied like tourniquets on all limbs. Didn't look like a friend to me. He reached for one of the cloth ties, pulled it down, and revealed a branding. A sort of poorly executed, self-inflicted tattoo. The letters "EF" etched in leathery skin.

"My contact?"

"No. A messenger," he said. "Make like you're going to the hovercraft dock, like you're going home for the night. Then double back and duck in the side door to the kitchen." His eyes trailed across the room to the door in question. My eyes followed.

He squeezed a hand against my neck to make it seem like he was an aggressor. Necessary for setting Marco's men off track, I assumed. Then he fell back into the rowdy, pulsing mass on the dance floor.

I grabbed a taco off a table and crammed it into my mouth, then dance-walked over to the hovercraft dock. I strolled onto the platform, into the crazy hum. Hover ships crisscrossed the setting sun, swarming in apparent disorder like bees in a garden.

"Uptown?" a blue suit asked me. Her red hair glistened in the sun's dimming rays.

"Yeah," I said. She smiled. The hovercraft pulled in. She stepped on. I stepped in after her. We brushed shoulders, then I remembered.

"Wait! I'm, uh, still hungry." I smiled apologetically. "One more taco should do the trick." I slipped off the ship. Its doors closed. Blue suit was whisked into the sky.

Back into the canteen, slinking low, lost in the throbbing mass of dancers. Moving along the wall, past a row of diners. To the swinging door.

Whoosh!

I was inside a dimly lit kitchen. Empty, though the still-wet floor reeked of bleach.

The door clapped shut, muting the after-work revelry of Yeerk happy hour. I moved through the pantry. No one. Into the main kitchen. Prep counters. Ranges. Refrigerators.

I froze. Labored breathing.

A kind of struggle for air through lungs that were seriously not well. I swung around and there, next to the island chopping block, was a wheelchair.

In the wheelchair, a woman. I'm not sure how I knew it was a woman. The face and body were grossly disfigured by injuries. She had no legs. Only one arm. A horrifying scar shut one eye.

The other eye looked up at me. It gleamed a brilliant blue.

I think I knew right then because the hair on the back of my neck stood on end.

"Aahhh Nihhh Morfff," came a sound from lips that barely moved. A scraping voice, harsh as railroad brakes, weak as a whisper. Yet strangely animated.

Animorph. The password!

Relief washed over me. A sudden wave. I was in the presence of a friend. It was about time! This pitiable woman . . . just a clever disguise.

"You don't even rec . . ." Thick wheezing cut off her words. She started up again. "You don't recognize me."

The arduous puffs of speech . . . this was no disguise.

"Cause I'm not kicking . . . Yeerk butt, you don't . . . even recognize . . . your own cousin?"

A sprig of dulled golden hair tucked behind a battered ear.

Reckless vitality still shining in her one eye.

"Cassie said you were dead!" I blurted.

She jammed her hand on the wheelchair joystick and lurched forward, stopping aggressively an inch from my boot.

"Close," she whispered. "But not quite."

CHAPTER 21

Rachel!

Not dead. Alive.

I couldn't find words. There were plenty racing around in my head, but none made it out. I just dropped to my knees and looked into her face. She had been so badly hurt. I wanted to ask how — why didn't she morph to repair the damage? But I was afraid of the answer.

I knew it was my doing. I knew I'd finally wasted Rachel's life.

"We don't do pity," she snapped, answering the expression on my face. "This is business. The serious stuff."

I nodded.

Why had Cassie lied to me?

105

"Eight blocks away is . . . the New York Public Library. A big abandoned building you . . . can't miss. Get there. Make the trip . . . from here to there the crookedest . . . line you can. We want them off . . . the scent."

I nodded again. It was hard for me to listen to her wheezing, but it didn't seem to bother her much at all.

"Go in . . . the side entrance," she continued. "Up two flights. Down . . . the hall and into the stacks. And wait."

"For what?"

"We don't do questions."

Suddenly —

Whoosh!

An Orff flung open the swing door. Shone his amber eye-light on pots, pans, me, stacked dishes. Back to me.

"Explain your position, Orange Suit."

Rachel's chair was low enough to the ground that he couldn't see her behind the island chopping block, but I was standing.

"I wanted more salsa. The tacos are bland," I said.

He thought a moment. I stared him down.

But when he stepped through the door my heart pounded. Maybe he was a figment of my subconscious, but pain was pain. Fear was fear. Marco had a point.

"Get the sauce," he bellowed, "and bring it to my table. You're right, the tacos stink."

He turned and walked out.

"They'll trail you," Rachel said. "At least now you know . . . who you need to lose."

"But do I meet someone? I want to do this right. Who do I look for? How will I know them?"

"You'll know." An undercurrent of the old enthusiasm carried her voice, even through the labored speech. "Believe me, you'll know."

I moved to leave. Her hand grabbed my suit.

"Don't let us down, Jake. It's not just . . . our freedom in the balance . . . this time. It's . . . life itself. There are many more . . . like me. Injured or weak or different. So let's do it . . . and do it right."

She released me. I wish I could say it didn't bother me to look at the mess Rachel had become, but it did. And in my mind, her wounds chronicled my failures as a leader. It was more than I could bear.

Without a backward glance, I swung through the door and back into the rowdy canteen. I couldn't tell exactly who was watching, but I felt the threat. I felt the stare of Marco's men.

A gravity lift dropped me at street level. Me and a group of blue suits looking to start a brawl with a Taxxon gang. I left them on the corner and started to move.

Down an alley. Back onto a main street. Another alley . . .

I needed to morph. I focused on the image of a peregrine falcon. I waited for my bones to start shrinking, the ground to start racing up at me.

Nothing happened. The changes didn't come!

I heard footsteps behind me. I looked back, but saw no one. Could Marco's men have some antimorphing technology?

I broke into a jog, dodging in and out of blown-out storefronts, doubling back on my tracks.

All the while I felt eyes on me. I saw no one. Just felt eyes.

And heard footfalls. When I slowed, they slowed. When I sped up, they followed.

I kept trying to morph, but the changes wouldn't come. Maybe it was me. Maybe my mind was too fragmented to focus.

In the middle of Forty-second Street, in the center of the path the Yeerks had cut through debris from the explosion, I stopped suddenly, waited two seconds, and spun around.

My boot struck the pavement. It was the sound of triumph. Because I'd captured exactly what I wanted.

I'd seen the Orff before they'd dimmed their eyes.

There was one on a first-floor balcony a half-block away, purple. And there was a group of three, crouched next to a junked hovercraft, their eyes red.

One of them was not even twelve feet away. A glowing orange follow spot. Invisible now, in the night, but that didn't matter. I'd charted it on my mental map.

Five total. I would lose these guys. I'd lose them without morphing. For Rachel.

Ready, set . . .

Gone! I pumped my legs. Worked them like springs, jumping over the debris-laden street and across the pavement. A powerful body in top condition. A host any Yeerk would give five ranks to get.

I couldn't see the Orff, but I could hear them. A fluid swishing followed by a thump, as each leg struck the ground. Swish-thump. Swish-thump. Swish-thump. Blending together so fast it was one sound. One rhythm. The Orff's three legs. Like a well-oiled engine.

I turned into another alley. Swish-thump. Only one Orff was near. But how close? I twisted and caught a glimpse. It was Orange-eye. Sticking to me. He wouldn't let me pull away.

I'd have to take this chase inside.

CHAPTER 22

I dove through the storefront, its sheet glass already blown out. I landed on a bed of sports equipment. Hockey skates jabbed my ribs. Sneakers broke my fall.

I raced to the back of the store. Boxes of shoes and skates and hockey pads piled high, overturned, spilled randomly across the floor. I tripped through the obstacle course, heading for the backstairs when . . .

Whoosh!

The floor in front of me was opening up! I couldn't stop. Moving too fast . . .

A black hole!

"Ahh!"

I grabbed for a shoe rack. It tumbled.

I was falling!

Like Alice in Wonderland, I was shooting through blackness. Or down a water park slide. Only beneath me wasn't a stream of H_2O, but a current of air so strong it kept me buoyant.

Air flew past so fast I could hardly breathe. I scratched the sides for a handhold, but they were smooth.

A twisting turn! Then flatness. Then a thirty-foot drop!

"Oh-wah-oh-wa-weh-se-gunta-go . . ."

<Oh-wah-oh-wa. . .>

What the . . . ?!

Kids. A mix of oral and thought-speak voices. Singing!

It was the first joyful sound I'd heard since waking in my cell.

I saw the end of the tunnel speeding toward me. No way to slow down!

"Yahhh!"

I was flying through night air, through a sky dotted by stars and warmed by the full moon.

Whumph!

An unexpectedly soft landing on a wide, grassy field. Next to me was a tree. But not just your average neighborhood maple or oak. This sucker was huge. A billowing, thriving tree whose branches bowed to touch the ground, then headed back up toward the sky. Like the baobabs of Africa I've seen on the Discovery Channel.

Every branch had a child on it. A smiling, playful child, singing and swaying. Some of them were obviously skilled tree-climbers. Not all of them were human, although most were. There were young Andalites, too. Even a number of Orff. And a Leeran.

"Oh-wah-oh-wa-weh-se-gunta-go!"

The singing stopped.

On the grass not far from me, beneath the tree, were some adults. A few were standing, others sat cross-legged. They didn't wear the colored suits of the Yeerk metropolis. Instead they had on loose-fitting, linen-colored tunics. A bulge in a pouch on their sides revealed handheld Dracons, but I got the feeling the weapons weren't used very often.

Adult Andalites stood thoughtfully nearby. A single Orff, barely visible in the darkness, crouched on his third leg while he extended the other two legs comfortably out in front of him.

A human female raised her hands with pleasure and smiled at the kids in the tree. "Very nice," she said. "We'll start the meeting now."

All heads turned up to the starry sky. An adult Andalite stepped forward.

<With it we walk, think, and speak. For it we breathe, sleep, and work.>

"Freedom guides us," everyone answered.

<For it we live.>

"Freedom is all."

Heads dropped. A human male asked the kids if they wanted to share what they'd worked on during the week. The female who'd led the song walked over to me.

"What is this place?" I asked. "Are you the group Cassie told me about? Are you free?"

"Yes. So Cassie sent you?"

"Well, no. I mean, I don't know. I just fell through a hole in the floor and . . ."

"The floor doesn't open up for just anyone. Cassie must want you to learn. You see, all our young adults are in the EF. We're the ones they've saved so far. We elders, and the children that we raise and teach." She pointed back at the tree. It must have been art week because each child had a painting of his own creation in his hands. The canvases were small, but intricate. One student at a time explained his work while the others listened.

"These are the first healthy kids I've seen since I've been here."

The woman nodded and squeezed my arm.

"It's a sad story, to be sure. I'll tell you." She

lowered her voice a notch. "The Yeerks raise children in large warehouses back in the city. Controllers like the ones you saw are picked at random to procreate. When children are born, they enter one of the wamps, or warehouses, where they are held from birth to age fifteen. Their lives are controlled though their brains are left uninfested. Children are seen as weak and unworthy host bodies.

"During this captivity," she continued, "they're pumped full of vitamin supplements so the host bodies will grow strong. They're run on treadmills so they'll be fit to fight and to produce. When instinct leads them to indulge in moments of uncontrolled, regular childhood, they are punished. If they try to educate themselves, they are punished. Yeerks want minds as powerless as possible. So they raise children in a joyless, lifeless world where they wait for the day of infestation. The EF fights to free them. When they are freed, which is far more seldom than I can bear to think, they come here."

"These kids don't seem traumatized at all," I said. "They seem completely normal."

"We've been lucky that way. Very few have been broken down beyond repair. This is a place of joy. It helps that we don't talk about the wamps unless we must. We live simply. We teach and cultivate. We hope."

She turned back to the class in progress, then back to me.

"Would you like to see more?"

I nodded. I felt it was important to see how things worked here. I felt that I was here because I was supposed to be.

CHAPTER 23

I walked over to the tree.

"Are you from the EF?" A kid's voice. I looked down at one of the lower, swooping branches and saw a blond, rosy-cheeked boy. Maybe eight or nine. He spoke like he hoped I was with the EF because that would make me a quasi-celebrity and someone worth showing his artwork to.

"Um, I guess so," I said. "Yeah. I'm working with the EF. My name's Jake."

"My name's Justice. The elders insist on giving us these funny 'concept' names. Like, that's Liberty over there." He pointed to a girl on a high branch. "And that's Storm." As he explained this, he rolled his eyes a little, indicating that to him, all adults seem a bit goofy.

116

I smiled and knelt down to get closer to his level.

"You want to see my painting?" he said. "My friends think I'm better at art than they are. The elders say I have a gift."

"Well, then, I'd better have a look."

Justice handed his canvas to me.

"What do you think?"

The image was divided diagonally, from the lower left corner to upper right. Below that line was an expressionist nightmare. A dark, angular city. Jutting, steel-gray towers rising through a bloodred mist. A fog from which arms and screaming, agonized faces reached in vain for a sky they couldn't see.

Above the diagonal demarcation was a different world. A cloudless, blue-skied landscape. In the sky hovered a hot-air balloon, stark-white, like a sun. Extending from the balloon's gondola, crossing over from the joyful sky to the dismal, urban abyss was a rope.

A cord, thin as thread.

On this rope were people, traveling upward, pinned to the thread like clothes on a laundry line.

And as they crossed the border between darkness and light, faces stiff with frustration and rage softened. There were no smiles, but there were expressions of hope.

117

"Do you like it, Jake?"

"It's great," I said. He smiled. "You're really good at drawing. Is that how you got here? Did you escape up the rope?"

"Not you too," he said with mild frustration. "The elders are always telling me I paint allegories, whatever they are! I'm working out my aggression and fears, they say. But I'm just painting what I want to."

"Okay."

"Do you get to fly Bug fighters?"

"Nope."

"But you get to plan attacks, right? And lead rebels? And free slaves?"

"I guess so."

"That's what I want to do. I'm gonna free all the friends I had to leave behind. They're prisoners and I'm gonna save them."

I wondered how I should answer, how I could explain to him, without destroying his spirit. "War doesn't always let you save the people you know," I said. "You might end up being assigned to a mission that saves people far away from here. People you don't know. Other people's friends."

He shook his head.

"I'll save my friends first. Then I'll save other people's friends." He jumped suddenly and grabbed hold of my arm, pulling me toward the trunk of the massive tree.

"You're gonna be late," he said. "I want you to stay, but you're gonna be late." He pressed his small hand on a depression in the thick, corrugated bark and a door appeared. It opened for me and I let Justice push me through it, but then I turned back.

When I did, there was just the trunk of an oak.

No door, no free humans.

I was back in the city.

In Bryant Park, awash in shadows from a nearly full, rising moon. Gnarled branches on leafless trees spread like outstretched hands. Hands warning of danger. Pleading with me to be careful.

Gravel crunched beneath my boots as I crossed to the New York Public Library. My mind hummed with confusion as I tried to make sense of the place I'd just been, the free humans I'd just met.

I'd decided a while back to give up analyzing what was happening to me and why. I'd figured that sanity depended on accepting the reality I saw, this dream or nightmare or vision. But that didn't mean there weren't times when all I wanted were answers — definite, concrete answers.

I listened for the sound of Orff footfalls. For the feel of spying eyes tracking me.

Nothing. I'd lost them.

I'd done as Rachel had said.

Up white marble steps.

"TSSEEERRR."

A raptor's cry cut the night. Then beating wings and the creaking of ancient bones.

"Tobias!"

Feathers brushed my face as a hawk shot past. So close this time! I blinked and . . .

Gone! Absorbed by the night.

"Tobias?" There was no answer.

So I turned and opened the massive, brass-handled door. I raced up moonlit stairs, boots pounding in the vast emptiness.

A wood-paneled corridor led to the stacks, to endless rows of high, book-lined shelves. A gloomy, moody maze. A musty, unlived-in smell. Silent as a tomb.

Reading obviously wasn't big with the Empire.

I walked along the main corridor, looking down each aisle. Rachel said I'd know.

I was in the beginning of the "E" section when I passed an aisle that seemed to extend farther than the rest. I turned into the book-lined tunnel, heart thumping, and began to run.

Suddenly, the bookshelves ended. I skidded

to a halt next to a row of dark-stained wooden tables. And then a hundred lights switched on and splashed light across the surfaces of a hundred desks, illuminating a huge reading room.

A strapping Andalite, coarse blue fur drawn tight over battle-ready muscles, swiveled graceful stalk eyes to rest on me.

<Jake.>

The thought-speak voice was mind-filling. Gentle and tough. Wise, inspiring, terrifying.

Familiar.

He looked just as he did the night his spacecraft crashed in the construction site. The night my life changed forever.

By comparison, my voice sounded puny and forlorn, swallowed up by the vaulted chamber.

"Elfangor."

CHAPTER 24

The Andalite shifted on his hooves and trotted nearer, his stature breathtaking. He was powerful and well-proportioned.

<You have followed our instructions.>

I'd seen Elfangor murdered with my own eyes, yet there he stood. Could he be leader of the EF? Mastermind of a terrorist campaign against Yeerk control? I was incredulous, but, at this point, anything seemed possible.

"The EF is certainly a force to be reckoned with," I said.

<It sounds as though you question our tactics.>

"Action is the surest path to change. No question there."

<But you would fight them differently? Sabotage and terrorist offensives make you morally uneasy. You want a better way.>

"What I want is to go home."

<Too much for you?> Elfangor was an awesome presence. I'd be lying to say he didn't intimidate me some. But I was a leader, too. I saw the fight for Earth as more mine now than his. I wanted to be respectful of him, but in my view he'd made a giant mistake with the terrorist campaign. I had to call him on it.

"No. I want to go home so I can keep all this from happening in the first place. If this is the future, I want to go back. I can stop the Yeerks without sacrificing my friends. Without botching the war, and bumbling into your brand of terrorism and half-freedoms. I can stop them before we sacrifice the very things we're fighting for!"

Elfangor laughed in my mind. <Victory without sacrifice? You know better than that.>

"You don't have to give up your principles to win. Isn't there always an alternative to sacrifice if you just keep your mind clear, and step back, and see it and . . ."

<You know better than that.>

The repetition stung. How did he know I was just talking big? It was like he was inside my head, rifling through my personal file of fears and mistakes . . .

Now I was angry.

"It's all your fault," I said suddenly, surprising myself. "I always thought of you as a hero, Elfangor. A leader. But the truth is you couldn't see another way out. You sentenced us to hardship, pain, and suffering. We were kids. You made us question every value we ever learned. You had no right to heap that weight on us, huge and impossible. You used us!"

<That's interesting, coming from you, Jake.> The voice changed as he said my name. Suddenly, he didn't sound like Elfangor anymore. The Andalite arrogance was gone, leaving only the voice of a man. A human. Familiar and unfamiliar.

<Let me guess what comes next,> the new voice said. <You didn't ask for leadership, right? You didn't ask to make the tough calls. Plan the missions. Decide how to use your small but loyal force. How and when to put them in harm's way, risking their lives. You're blameless. The role was thrust upon you. Well, I don't buy it, Jake. Every choice is yours. Always has been. You were and are free.>

"Tobias."

<Yeah. You know I morphed Ax a long time ago. I decided to stay in this morph. Ax's body has aged ten years. It's a dead ringer for Elfangor, isn't it? But Elfangor's dead, Jake.>

Of course.

<And so are you.>

My throat tightened. My skin tingled. What? My mind seized on his words, pulled and prodded them. Turned and shook them.

Dead? Then how could I be free?!

<Ten years ago tonight, Tom put it all together. He came into your room and murdered the leader of the Animorphs. Rather than let Visser Three know that one of the notorious "Andalite bandits" had gone undetected for so long, right under his nose, Tom ended your life. Your own brother . . . >

"But I'm here!"

I looked down at my hand. Pink-tan flesh under the light of the reading lamp. Knuckles, nails, veins, bones. Alive. Real.

<Yes, you're here, but not alive.>

What was this?

<It all converges tonight. Battles, struggle, strategy. Tonight is the decisive moment. The Chrysler Building moon ray is ready for use. They're powering it up as I speak. Running through the checklist. Applying your hundreds of hours of calculations.>

"No! No, no, no! I'm not a scientist!"

<You are. You were. Or rather, you will be. It all rests on you. You're the only one . . . only you can make the shot miss. Get there, Jake. Alter

the programming. Make it miss. Even a tenth of a percent will do the job. This is the decisive moment, do you understand? Use whatever means necessary.>

"If I make the shot miss, the moon will explode and doom millions."

<The greater good, Jake. The big picture. For God's sake, don't get stopped by details. Permanent Kandrona. Failure means an Earth that is at last irrevocably Yeerk.>

"But what about Cassie? Marco has her!"

<There's no time. She's prepared to die with honor.>

"Couldn't you send someone else to save her? One of your people?" I pleaded, indignant at his dismissal of her life.

Tobias shrugged.

<No one to spare.>

"I won't let her die!"

<Save one or save many? The choice wasn't so hard for you at the Ragsin Building, when you left Marco and Rachel to save themselves.>

I couldn't answer that.

<This is war, Jake. Sacrifices must be made.>

He turned abruptly and walked across the room.

<Alter the moon ray or save Cassie. One or the other. Or neither. Not both.>

CHAPTER 25

I couldn't accept it.

I ran out the same way I came in, as fast as my legs could carry me. Past row upon row of books and cavernous marble library halls built for a different world.

I burst out into a muggy cloud of night air, thick and hot. The leaves on the trees were full and lush. Leaves? Muggy air? Minutes ago I'd walked beneath barren branches, dormant as death. Now I raced past foliage rustling in the whirlwind currents from hovercraft overhead.

Reality was all wrong.

Cassie.

No mission was worth sacrificing her life.

I ran from Tobias. From Elfangor and Ax, from friends who'd ceased to care.

As leader of the Animorphs, I would put the mission first. The mission as a whole. But what was my mission?

What made the world worth more? Sheer volume? The future? The common good?

Detachment, you idiot.

The last battle we'd fought together . . . Marco and Rachel, inside . . . lose everyone or just two . . . a door closing . . . Securing their destiny . . .

Guilt tore at me with scratching, ripping claws.

I'd set the example. I was to blame for Cassie's hardness and Tobias's indifference.

I ran still faster. Down a dark, narrow backstreet. The smell of Taxxon filth invaded every corner of the city. Sweat poured down my face, mixing with burning, unstoppable tears.

"I'm sorry!" I shouted at the sky.

No one to hear.

Tobias was wrong about war. What good is it if people are forgotten along the way? If one girl in one million girls is scarred and hardened. Changed forever. What good? Only Yeerks freely give their own to see a job completed. I wasn't a Yeerk.

I wasn't.

TSEEEW!

A flash of heat. The scorch of Dracon fire on the bricks above my face.

Marco's men!

Get away! I had to get above this nightmare town! I tore at my synthetic orange skin and tried to morph.

The physical changes began. I hadn't lost the morphing power! Long human legs collapsed up into my rear. Elbows fused to my chest.

A downy undercoat sprouted across my skin. Stiff feathers shot outward from thinning arms. Hard cranial bones shifted, sculpting my heavy, round human head into the falcon's sleek form.

I flapped as hard as I could. Struggling through wet air.

Help Cassie, and I doom so many more. Kandrona for eternity. Help Cassie and mankind's fate is sealed.

But I would have one more moment with Cassie by my side. We might make it. We could run.

But where could we go? And with a Kandrona sun, I couldn't even starve the Yeerk out of her head . . .

Every detail of the city surged into focus with raptor sight. And the mind. Simple, but keen. Focused on the task. No swells of emotion. No unanswered questions.

The tears were gone.

Higher. Past walls of silver-green glass and rooftop landing pads. Glassed-in penthouses, beacons in the darkness, housed crowds of humans and Andalites gathered around sludgy pools. High-level Controllers cavorting and conspiring. The alien world's hot tub equivalent. The Yeerk pool.

The air cooled and thinned as I rose higher still, until at last, the menacing Yeerk New York looked safe and small. Air began to slip past my tired wings. I was an insignificant dot in the sky. One free soul above a city of slaves. Millions that were mine to save.

Cassie.

Justice would save his friends first.

But Justice was a kid.

CHAPTER 26

The lights of Yeerk and once-Andalite craft flitted over streets like crimson fireflies. Brooklyn. Queens. The Bronx. The suburbs. The string of distant cities beyond. All of it glowed a telling red. The East Coast megalopolis, to the horizon and beyond.

Yeerk. All of it. Yeerk.

My telescopic falcon eyes found the silhouette of a man at a desk, high in a skyscraper. In the world I used to know, he could have been anyone. Working late. With a wife and a family. A dog. A home.

Here he was a captive. One captive.

One life.

Two miles away was another building, not the

131

tallest, but one that stood out, with a pointed, shining peak. Brighter than all the structures around it, with starbursts stacked to form a tall, elegant tip.

The Chrysler Building. Center of the invaders' command. Instrument of Yeerk domination.

Cassie's prison.

A stunning yellow light electrified the massive peak. The needle rod planted at the top began to pulse.

Then suddenly, right before my eyes . . . the giant metallic gargoyle eagles that jutted from the corners of the spire's base seemed to ignite!

The moon ray was energizing.

An emerald-green glow was growing within the eagles, emanating, gaining intensity.

Shafts of green sprang from the eagle heads, like controlled lightning. Rose up and up, converging at the spire's needle tip!

A pyramid of green with an axis of gold, all of it sizzling energy!

I pulled in my two-foot wings and began the dive. Thirty, forty, fifty miles an hour. The Chrysler Building my prey.

I plummeted through cold air, faster and faster. Eighty, ninety . . . a feathered bullet. A dark streak in the night.

And then, a detail.

A human form! A woman, perched on a narrow ledge a thousand feet from the ground, one of the giant gargoyles anchored just beneath her feet! She was facing out, away from the building, her wrists strapped to the masonry wall, her face strained as she fought to break free.

<CaaaaSieeeee!>

She twisted.

<The spire!> Her desperate plea filled my head. <Smash the spire!>

How could she answer in thought-speak? How could she even see me? No time to wonder.

The building was racing toward me. The green beams were growing wider and wider, expanding toward Cassie's perch. They'd fry her! In seconds, she'd be toast.

<The smallest misalignment will disable it!> she screamed. <Smash into the spire! Do it now!>

Razor talons could tear away Cassie's bonds. Free, she could take cover from the beams. She could survive.

<The spire!>

Indecision slowed my thoughts, and my descent.

The Chrysler Building glowed brighter and brighter. The air vibrated with turbulence. The ray seemed desperate to activate. An endless supply of Kandrona. An Earth forever Yeerk.

One well-placed impact — a five-pound falcon traveling at top speed — and the whole operation might fail. Two lives given to save millions more. To save Earth's future . . .

Cassie yanked at the living bonds that held her wrists. She fought them, bit them, banged them against the wall. All she could do until suddenly . . .

<Ahhhhh!> She was free!

And then she leaped forward. Jumped from the brick ledge to the base of the gargoyle, perilously close to the raging green shaft. Slammed her weight onto the eagle. It quaked minutely, but it was enough. The light dimmed!

<You did it!> I cheered. The spire's color weakened from blinding white to dull yellow.

<No! I only misaligned an auxiliary stabilizer. The system will be up and running again in minutes!>

Before I could respond, a panel hissed open behind her. Strong, nearly invisible Orff arms enveloped her.

<Jake! Disable the main computers!>

She was dragged inside. And the panel shut. Except for a crack.

CHAPTER 27

A scarlet slit. The only entrance to the Yeerk fortress.

I braked hard against the incredible force of a full dive. The narrow vertical opening approached too fast. I'd miscalculated.

The only solution, maybe, was a fierce bank. One wing tip stretched at the ground, the other to the sky. I flattened my body. Braced for impact.

Whhhhumpppppfffff.

My hollow bird bones were crushed as momentum forced the falcon's too-large body through the slit.

Wham!

I smacked a marble wall. Dropped to the cool stone floor.

Stay conscious, Jake. My body was shattered, unresponsive. Blackness closed in, blurring my vision.

Feebly, I looked back at the narrow slit. Was I hallucinating? Perched atop the gargoyle-eagle, was a real bird. A red-tailed hawk. Eyes on me.

<Demorph.> The strong voice pulled me back.

My human form. Human . . .

Miraculously, splintered bones began to fuse and grow. Fly, kill, eat, protect. The raptor's calming elemental instincts were forgotten by the confused human mind.

<It's not too late.> The same strong voice.

I got up. I followed the sound of Cassie's kicks against the corridor. The building vibrated as the moon ray powered up again.

So little time.

I remorphed as I ran, bounding silently toward a red panel at the end of the hall on big Siberian paws.

Ka-blam!

I slammed the barrier and the half-inch-thick alloy easily folded. The door ripped from its track and revealed an immense chamber aglow with computer screens.

Four armed Orff on high platforms.

Two rows of Hork-Bajir.

And a voice raging from above.

"You again!"

It was Marco, glaring down from a pedestal hovering high in the center of the room, enclosed by a semicircular control panel fused to the base.

A large holographic display at the front of the room showed an image of the moon.

Displayed beside this moon view was a live image of the Chrysler Building. The spire glowed white-hot. Numbers beneath ticked away the seconds. 00:28. 00:27.

"Don't even bother trying," Marco boasted. "Neither of you can do anything to stop this." He motioned to the wall of windows, where Cassie, bound and gagged, struggled in vain.

"In minutes, the moon will shine and strengthen only Yeerks. We will be all-powerful. Earth will be ours forever."

A panel behind Cassie flew open, revealing a red night.

"And to celebrate, we've decided to throw a terrorist from the sky."

I sprang.

"Get him!"

TSEEEWW! TSEEEWW!

Dracon fire electrified the floor under my paws. Waves of Hork-Bajir moved in from every direction. I was hit! Hard, sharp blades sliced my back and neck. No pain. Not yet. I wouldn't let pain in. Not even as blood spewed from my cuts. Staining my fur. Coating my muzzle.

I fought back, wildly. Madly spilling purple-blue Hork-Bajir blood.

Five were down. A new wave rushed to catch me. No!

Propelled by hind legs like rockets, I sailed over the approaching attackers. Landed hard. Tumbled into two Orff.

"Get him, you morons!"

I slashed frantically. Sent their handheld Dracons flying like twigs in a hurricane.

I moved in to finish the job.

"Rrroooaaarrrr!"

The Orffs' clear, soft neck tissue yielded to my fangs like soft butter to a knife. But the taste!

I withdrew. Gagged and spat.

The poisonous, toxic taste!

Before I could recover one of the Orff closed his arms around my neck. Two legs clamped around my sides. The third kicked wildly at my gut.

I bit into the other Orff's leg, crushing arteries. Grinding leg bones in my jaw. Forcing myself to tolerate the taste.

He fell.

The one on my back increased his stranglehold. We were locked, Greco-Roman wrestlers who'd forgotten the rules.

The numbers beneath the hologram. 00:14. 00:13.

No!

Marco towered above, triumphant. Eyes fixed on the holograms. Fists clenched.

A scream!

Cassie! Hurled through the opening, into the red night!

BAAAM!

Violently, I rammed the Orff on my back against the wall.

BAAAM!

He struggled, resisted. Tried to choke me. Cut off my air.

BAAAM!

I smashed him again. His kicking slowed. His grip loosened.

He dropped to the floor, his green hearts spilling blood through severed vessels.

I looked at the window. Cassie.

And then, somehow, crazily . . . a hand reached up. Three fingers gripped the ledge. Cassie's hand. She wasn't gone! But in seconds she would tumble to her sixty-story death, a splattered heap for Taxxons to lick up.

In seconds the moon ray would fire, shooting from the Chrysler Building cannon with perfect aim and precision.

Cassie's hand.

The large, red button standing out on Marco's control panel, shielded behind glass. The word ABORT etched on the cover.

139

Cassie . . .

The world . . .

I knew what I had to do. No time for indecision. I saw my goal.

Save what should be valued above all else.

I leaped.

00:05. 00:04.

CHAPTER 28

I NTERESTING CHOICE.

All was blackness when I heard the voice.

A strange voice. Old and young. Male and female. Echoing in my mind like distant thought-speak.

It was not the Ellimist. No. It was a voice I'd never heard.

THEY HAVE STRANGELY SEGMENTED MINDS: CONSCIOUS, UNCONSCIOUS, AND AN ABILITY TO RECONCILE BOTH. THEY WILL BEAR MORE STUDY, THESE HUMANS . . .

A bird's song.

Bright sun on my face. Warmth.

I opened my eyes.

A wooden desk with a computer on it. *Star*

Wars Episode I poster tacked to the wall. School-books heaped on the floor. Dirty clothes falling from the closet. Worn gym shoes. Reading light. Cotton sheets.

Downstairs, the smell of fresh waffles cooking. Dad. A woman talking about a doubles game. Mom.

My room. My house. My . . .

I leaped out of bed.

The Schwarzenegger thing was history. My hand was my hand again. I brushed my chin. No sandpaper. Just smooth.

I grabbed for the phone. I dialed the number. Pounded the keypads. My body ached in muscles I didn't know I had.

Brrrrrrrr-ing.

Come on. Pick up.

Brrrrrrrr-ing.

Answer!

I wanted to hear a girl's voice. Deep and young. Cheerful and wise.

My heart pounded.

Bright sun washed my body. I moved a hand across my chest and felt . . .

My badge! I yanked it off.

I looked.

My fingers clutched air. I opened my fist. Nothing.

Images still flashed through my head.

Dead Hork-Bajir towering above me.

Orff manacling my wrists.

David.

A mind-blowing explosion.

The Howler.

The strangely beautiful singing of children.

The stench of those condemned to death.

A Mylar sheath beating with the wind.

The scarred faces and mangled bodies of old friends.

Elfangor.

Lightning. Rain. Slipping . . .

Brr . . .

"Hello?"

Time stopped.

Everything got extremely quiet. Except for the pounding of my heart.

I knew now. I'd made a choice. I knew what I was made of. My limitations and priorities.

"It's Jake," I said.

No response.

"It's Jake," I said again, voice quaking like I'd never talked to her before.

As if this were the first call I'd ever made. The only call that mattered.

"Cassie, I just wanted to ask what I should have asked you yesterday. Are you okay?"

O Most Powerful Emperor, Lord of the Galaxy! Bad news. Our ship's engines have again malfunctioned! The treacherous popinjay males pushed the red button instead of the blue one! Weaker and less worthy servants would be vanquished by this disaster! But the brave Helmacron females are undaunted! We alone will capture the blue box of transforming power! All the galaxy shall tremble before us, rightful leaders of our race!

— From the log of the Helmacron Females

Tseeew! Tseeew!

I felt two pinpricks on my neck. Like mini mosquito bites. "Ahhh! Owww!"

Maybe it was the lack of sleep, but I was already extremely ticked off. I wanted to pop those little jerks.

"The Helmacrons," Marco said with an amazed shake of his head. "I can't believe some-

one hasn't blasted these maniacs out of the uni-
verse by now."

The Helmacrons are a race of tiny aliens.
About a sixteenth of an inch tall, tops. But it's a
sixteenth of an inch of egomania. They sound
pretty harmless, right? Wrong. They have this
shrinking ray. The technology to make you very,
very tiny. To bring you down to their size.

This makes them both annoying and dangerous.

<You would have the Lords of the Universe
wait?> the Helmacron voice in my head blus-
tered. <We demand the power source! And we
demand it now! Follow our orders and live as our
debased swine! Or resist us and be blasted into
twisted molecules! See our might. Learn to obey
your new masters!>

"I don't get it," Jake said. "We already gave
them one jump start. Why are they here again?"

"Who cares?" I asked. "Let's just get rid of
them."

"Maybe something went wrong with their ship,"
Cassie said. "Hey — where are they going?"

The Barbie mobile backed up, did a 180, and
zipped toward the back of the barn.

"Let's go!" Marco said.

We got up and trotted after them. I could hear
Tobias flapping above us. We caught up in time

to see the truck's rubber tires bounce off a battered freezer chest in one of the empty stalls.

Jake met Cassie's eyes. "Is it in there?"

"Yes."

"It" was the blue box. That's what we call it. The Andalites have another name for it. Several actually. Anyway, it's the device they use to transfer the morphing power to an individual. Kind of like a super-advanced alien battery. Elfangor used it on us.

Last time we saw the Helmacrons, we made a deal with them. They could use the blue box to power up their engines. Then they had to get off Earth. Pronto. And stay off Earth. Forever.

Obviously, they hadn't kept their half of the bargain.

<They're cutting into the freezer!> Tobias announced.

I couldn't see anything, but hawks have amazing vision. You'd have to have outstanding eyesight to see what the Helmacrons were doing with their tiny energy beams.

Cassie shot a nervous look over her shoulder. "My dad doesn't need to see this."

"No problem," I said. I grabbed a pitchfork that was leaning up against the wall. "I'll get them."

"I'll help." Marco grabbed a ceramic pot. "I'm gonna trap these weirdos like bugs under glass."

We moved toward the freezer.

The pink-and-aqua truck spun around and raced right between us.

Marco pounced.

I pounced and jabbed the pitchfork down on top of the truck. Vaguely aware that my elbow had hit Marco and that he was stumbling backward, clutching his head.

So what? The Helmacron ship had rolled off the truck and was tumbling toward the freezer. All I had to do was grab it.

Out of the corner of my eye, I saw Marco lose his footing and trip.

"Get it!" Cassie screamed.

"Look out!"

THUNK!

Marco. Sliding down the side of the freezer. Slumping forward into the hay.

"What happened?" I demanded.

"Marco hit his head on the corner of the freezer," Jake said.

Cassie had already rushed to Marco's side. "Marco? Marco? Can you hear me?"

No reply. He was out cold.

"Man, these Helmacrons are bad news," I complained.

Jake raised an eyebrow. "Rachel, you were the one who elbowed Marco in the head."

"Because the little monsters were distracting me!"

<They're getting away!> Tobias shouted.

I glanced down. The Helmacron ship was right where it had fallen. I picked it up. "No worries," I said. "I've got them."

Tobias swooped toward Marco's head and narrowly missed grazing Cassie with his talons.

"Hey, watch out!" Cassie yelled.

<They're getting away.> Tobias repeated.

Then I got it. The Helmacrons had bailed out of their ship. They were loose somewhere in the barn.

"Where are they?" I demanded.

<Heading straight for Marco's nose!>

"What?" But I was already down on my knees, inches from Marco's face.

Frantically, I scanned the hay and dirt.

<Move!> Tobias ordered. <Get away from him so I can see.>

Cassie and I scrambled back.

<Oh, no,> Tobias said. <This is bad. Very, very bad.>

"What?" Jake demanded.

<They went up his nose,> Tobias said.

"How many?"

<About a dozen.>

<Hah-HAH!> one of the Helmacrons cried. <The vicious human attacks us with a mighty metallic weapon, but we are not defeated! Give

us the power source now and we will kill you quickly! Hesitate and we will prod you with sharp sticks before you die!>

"Give me one good reason why we should cooperate with you pipsqueaks," I demanded.

<Grovel and beg our forgiveness!> the Helmacron demanded. <Do as we say or your oblivious comrade will die!>

"News flash," I said. "Keep threatening us and you'll never get off Earth alive."

<Brave Helmacron females care nothing for their own safety!> the voice shouted. <We care only for glorious victory!>

<As do we, the newly liberated and courageous Helmacron males!> came another voice.

<We will kill the gigantic alien!> the first voice shouted.

<Not if we kill it first,> the second voice answered.

Then the Helmacrons fell silent. Probably beginning their march deeper into Marco's nose.

"What's this about male and female?" Jake asked.

Cassie shrugged. "Don't you remember? When the Helmacrons were here before, Marco and I kind of gave the males a little . . . pep talk. We didn't like the way the females were always bossing them around."

"Well, now the Helmacrons have even more cause to fight among themselves," Jake reasoned. Let's just hope they don't do too much fighting before we can figure out how to get them out of Marco's nose."

ANIMORPHS ®

K. A. Applegate

Step inside the World of

www.scholastic.com/animorphs

The official website

Up-to-the-minute info
on the Animorphs!

Sneak previews
of books and
TV episodes!

Contests!

Fun downloads
and games!

Messages from
K.A. Applegate!

See what other fans
are saying on the Forum!

It'll change the way you see things.